The Tears of Tyrra
Book 1

Memoirs of the Crimson Dwarf

by Feldspar Forgehammer Chilox

Black Axe Press

Copyright © 2007-2010 by Matthew Taylor
All rights reserved.

ISBN **978-1478110989**

Printed in the United States of America

Memoirs of the Crimson Dwarf

Also by Feldspar Chilox:
Tears of Tyrra Book 2: Memoirs of the Azure Elf

To Zenda

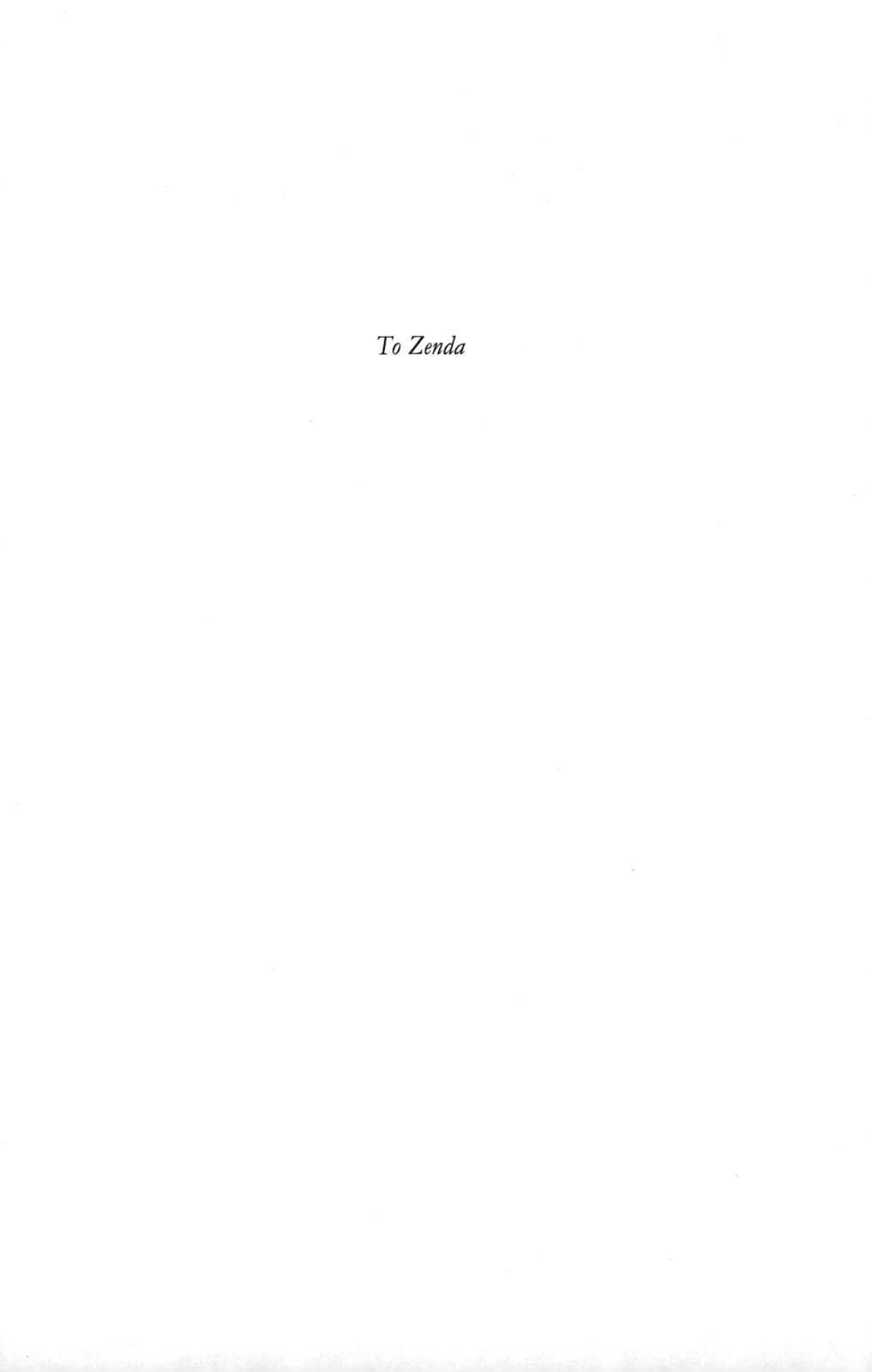

Dear reader,

As much as the next dwarf, I love to tell a tale over a mug of ale. I've been through so much in my one hundred twenty-three winters. I've often thought about telling my own tale, start to finish, as much as I can remember. I have left out little, though at times my boastfulness has gotten the better of me and my yarn has become more fiction than fact.

I owe an inestimable amount of gratitude to many people, including my thane, Taestiv Chilox, my cousin, Hiddukel Chilox, my friends and my fellow adventurers. I would also like to thank Bertold Fairoak, Rakella Leafdancer, Guildmistress Blindor Silverlode and Viscountess Willissa Entemoor Arkeel, who have given to me untold amounts of information about my heritage and my people's history, including a version of the story of King Ringold and Queen Nephtali which I have retold herein.

If I mentioned everyone to whom I owe gratitude for the publishing of these memoirs, this book would quickly turn into a copy of my Book of Debts. I've no wish to bore the non-dwarven people who might read this, but I would like to mention a few of those to whom I owe so much: Leafton "Decoy" Adirondak, your antics have saved my life more than once; the Asgards, may your courage never fail; Zenda, I still care for you, even though the poison's spell has faded.

Feldspar Chilox

14 August 607

A Lily

I hummed a tune to myself as I worked. No, not at the forge. I wasn't yet old enough to work the forge. My father had told me so. I was just going on my twenty-fifth summer. That was young for my people. The oldest dwarf I ever heard of was almost five hundred years old, and it was common for a person to live past three hundred, if he did not die by battle or accident.

"You need tae look after yer mum an' sis," my dad had said, "Yer brothers an' I'll work the metal. When you grow a beard longer than yer thumb, then you can learn the art." I checked the fuzz on my chin. The beard-growth stones that my brother sold to me weren't working. The wretch, he'd played the gypsy. I rubbed them against my face each day, but the hair was still barely as long as my thumb was wide.

It seemed as though it would be forever before I would see the glow of the steel that my father shaped into horseshoes, plows, and axes. I looked down at the small hatchet in my hands, a birthday gift from my father. I traced my fingers along the smooth, seamless head that betrayed no hammer marks. My father was a master at his art. He could make his work look like he hadn't spent hours slamming it around with a hammer, melting and remelting its surface until the metal blended like soft clay and ended up as smooth as silk and almost as hard as the stonewood.

No, not as hard as stone, as hard as stonewood. Stonewood is much harder than any rock I've ever felt. That was where most of Father's blades went; he sold them to the Woodcutter's Guild. They constantly needed new axe-heads because even blades as hard in temper as my father's could not last long when they were used to harvest the rock-like trees which gave our town its name, and its fortune. Like every young dwarf in the town, I dreamed of becoming a 'Cutter, wielding one of my father's axes, felling the tall stonewood trees, bringing in gold for my family.

"Then my da would respect me," I said to myself, "then he'd beg me to come to his forge. But I'd say, 'No, da, I must be gettin' back to work. The scouts've marked ten more trees for me.' Nay, an hundred, a thousand more trees. An' I'll fell 'em all." I swung the small hatchet, pretending that I was chopping down an army of the tallest of those living pillars.

I burst into tears. That would never happen. I'd never be a 'Cutter, and Dad would never let me work with him. He'd just keep on telling me, "Yer too young, Crimson Let the men do the man's work." I could be a thousand years old and still he'd tell me, "Yer brothers are more suited to the art; they're stronger and more skilled. Look after yer mum an' sis."

I threw the hatchet at the ground, burying its head halfway into the soft soil. Then, I ran. My feet carried me through brambles and thickets, my mind unseeing and unaware of my surroundings. I wanted to get out of there. Where could I go? I'd never been out of Stonewood. Maybe I could go live with the elves or something, or maybe I could go to the mountains and find my highland kin. They'd teach me to work the forge. They wouldn't think me too young or too weak.

A root caught my foot and the world spun around me. Everything was a blur until I landed with a thud, my head just missing a low branch.

I heard laughter behind me, giggling. I spun around. I couldn't see anything there except the trees. Gaining a hold on my fears, I turned my frightened look into a mask of strength, trying to imitate my father's meanest look.

"Who goes there? F-friend or foe?" I asked in my most fearsome voice, which cracked only slightly. "If ye be foe, I'll tear you apart, limb by limb." I squared my shoulders, trying to look mean and tough.

The gentlest of touches on my back startled me so much that I nearly leapt out of my boots. Once again, I found myself on the ground. Images of rampaging orcs filled my head as I huddled in the dirt, trying now to look even smaller than I was.

My fear was broken by a giggle. Orcs didn't giggle. They growled and belched and cursed and gnashed their teeth, but they didn't giggle. It was just some dumb girl playing a trick on me. I didn't know how she managed to sneak up on me so quietly, but I'd get her back somehow. The burning rush told me that my face was turning red, first from embarrassment, then from anger. I pulled myself slowly back to my feet before turning to face my molester.

My mouth opened of its own accord. The tall, slender, pale-skinned woman who stood in front of me was no dwarf-girl. Her skin had a slight greenish tint, like fresh buds in spring. She wore no clothing, but strategically placed vegetation prevented my young eyes from popping out of my head. Her hair was as red as autumn leaves and she wore a white flower behind one ear.

She must be a dryad. My father told stories about them. He and the woodcutters used to joke about them. Mother always yelled at Dad about it, but I was too young at the time to understand why. The dryads were said to be all through these woods, but you only saw one if she wanted you to see her. They were creatures of the forest, spirits of the trees, and the trees hid and protected them. In return, they nurtured all the plants and animals in the wood.

I looked into the dryad's deep green eyes and I felt encircled, caught in a silken web. It was not like the cold steel of a trap. It felt like being wrapped in a warm blanket on a winter's night. In that instant, the whole forest opened up to me. I could hear the rustling of the leaves in the wind and the songs of the birds in the canopy. For that moment, I wasn't in the forest; I was the forest, reaching upwards with my branches, trying to touch the sun, and, at the same time, stretching my roots into the earth, holding onto Tyrra.

She spoke, and the music of her voice washed over me, calming me, swallowing me in green eternity. Her laughter, like the bright chirping of finches, jingled in my heart and tickled it. Soon, I was laughing along with her.

There is a legend among the Stonewood folk that dryad blood flows through all of us. In fact, the legend claims that the stonewood trees were created by a king of my people, a mighty wizard who cast a powerful spell on the trees to preserve them and preserve the dryads who lived among them, so that he might spend the ages with the queen of the nymphs, whom he loved. In that moment, I truly believed that legend. I could feel the blood pumping through my veins, my heart beating with every word that floated from her strawberry lips.

"You must stay with me, young one." In her speech was the whispering of the wind. "I will protect you."

I did not think at the time to question her about why I would need protection. I only did what my spirit willed me to do: I grasped her delicately firm hand and followed, abandoning any outside thoughts.

Her name was Lillie, she explained to me. Her grip was surprisingly strong, despite her figure, so thin I could almost see through it, and so tall as to be ungainly. Her fingers were long, nearly twice the length of my own, but only half the width. Her skin appeared smooth and youthful, but it was rough to the touch.

Listening to the entire forest around me, I noticed that my feet barely made a sound. Dry leaves and twigs seemed to leap out of the way. My heavy leather boots, normally thumping loudly as I ran, seemed to float just above the ground. Or maybe the dirt softened beneath my tread, making my passage almost silent.

She led me to a patch of raspberries, not yet ripe. With a whispered word and a wave of her hand, the berries turned from green to red to a deep purple. They fleshed out and grew plump. Lillie picked one and held it out for me.

Giggling at my hesitation, she ate the first berry and picked another. She held this one out for me, too. I took it and looked at it carefully before I placed it in my mouth. It wasn't the right season for raspberries, but here was a whole bush of fruit that was perfectly plump, juicy, and ripe. It tingled in my stomach and that tingle spread outward, filling my whole body with a warm snugness.

It seemed like hours that I spent with Lillie, staring at the sky through the canopy. I felt a heavy weight when she told me I must leave.

"It is time for you to return," she said. "Your father needs you."

"Why would he need me?" I asked. "He's still at the forge, and he has my brothers to help him."

"Trust me." She gave me a reassuring smile as she reached up to her ear and removed the flower, placing it in my hands and closing my small fist around the stem. "He needs you."

I looked down at her hand, holding mine shut, and at the snowy blossom. With her urging, I turned towards home. When I looked back, she was gone; the empty forest took her place. No birds sang; no squirrels chattered. The wood was suddenly dark and quiet. I plodded down the path, hearing only the slap of my soles on the packed dirt.

It was not long before I reached the spot where I had left my hatchet. I pulled its muddy head out of the ground and carried it with me, my arm dangling lifelessly from my side.

The air was heavy, oppressive. My eyes were glued to my feet as they slowly took me home, one step at a time. I did not look up until I reached the town, clutching my hatchet in one hand and the flower in the other.

I smelled the smoke first. I scrunched up my nose against its acrid sting. My eyes began to water and every breath was thick and labored. When I finally forced myself to look up, tears streamed down my face and I was choking on the lump in my throat.

The flames licked up from my childhood. The bright orange azaleas my sister had grown from finger-sized clippings blazed yellow and red. The wire hutch my brother had built for his rabbits was ripped in two, crimson blood and silver fur clinging to the blackened steel. One half of the wooden facade still stood, torn by razor claws. My mother's stew pot lay overturned, dented by some massive club. The straw from the mattresses flared up on top of a shattered loom. The unfinished fabric, once white, was now stained with black, brown, and red. Only one thing was capable of such carnage: orcs.

In the center of the wreckage, on top of a section of the collapsed porch, his calloused hands white with exertion, my father held on to his last sliver of hope, the pale, delicate hand of his dead wife. In my hand, I grasped a small piece of infinity: a lily.

After that, my father took me to live with my grandparents in the Dwarfhaven Mountains. The journey was long and rough, riding in the back of the wagon that doubled as my father's traveling workshop. The road was filled with potholes and large stones, and I had only a wood plank to serve as a seat and a bed.

Even though we traveled in a caravan with the stonewood merchants, father wouldn't let me visit with any of them. I had to stay in the back and "mind the wares, boy." My two brothers rode up front with him, making my little heart burn with jealousy. I vowed to find some way to gain my father's favor, and knock down my brothers a couple notches while I was at it.

With sudden inspiration I peeled back the canvas that covered the floor of the wagon. Hidden under the floorboards of the wagon, my father kept a secret stash of orc bait. My father bought some of the most potent ingredients to make his orc bait, so he kept the final two parts of the chemical in separate containers. I pulled two bottles from the hiding place, covering my actions with the noise of the wheels hitting rocks. My dad and brothers would not hear much on this rough country road.

The bottles were old looking. They were slightly misshapen, not like the fine containers bartered from the elves these days. The glass was ruddy and dark, one bottle green, the other brown. The corks were sealed in with grey wax, so dark it was almost black.

It was hard to peel back the wax. I dug my fingernails under it and pried away, but it was fifteen minutes before I'd managed to uncover the cork of the first bottle. Using the small knife I carried for carving my meat, I pushed the cork down into the bottle.

The smell wasn't as bad as I had expected. I was sure that orc bait would smell horribly, like the orcs it was meant to attract, but it wasn't unpleasant. In fact, it smelled quite good. I dabbed a bit on my finger. It wasn't mixed with the chemical in the other bottle, so it wouldn't attract the orcs yet. I just wanted a closer inspection. It was a brownish yellow, and smelled kind of like those orange fruits the gypsies brought with them from the South, with a hint of cinnamon. My stomach rumbled. Those fruits were tasty, sweet and succulent. I wished I had one to eat, just a little bite.

The cart jolted over a big rock, awakening me from my daydream. I had been about to drink the substance. I shook my head. What had I been thinking?

"Pull y'self together, Crimson. This stuff's fer the orcs, not you, beardless fool." I started work on the second bottle.

Soon enough, both were open. I had only to mix them together, just a small amount. I pulled a small ring from my pocket. It was one of the mystical rings of dreaming that get passed around the town of Stonewood. The old women of the village know how to craft these tokens from the mud and moss taken from the base of stonewood trees. When worn, the rings hold fast to your finger for days or weeks, until you are granted a dream. They say the dreams have special significance, but I've never been any good at interpreting them.

Anyway, this ring had given me a dream: memories of my mother mixed with memories of the dryad, Lillie. The next morning, it had slipped from my finger. I was supposed to pass it on to another dwarf so that he could receive his dream, but this time it was going to bring more than a dream.

I spilled a couple drops from the first bottle onto the ring and grabbed the second bottle. This was the point of no return. Should I do it? Would it work? I envisioned myself coming to my brother's rescue as the orc charged after him with slavering jaws. A few drops from the second bottle finished the mixture and sealed my fate.

I put new corks in the bottles and hastily returned them to their hiding spot as the wagon came up upon our campsite for the night. I quickly grabbed a third bottle, which I knew contained the antidote, orc repellent. Returning the boards to their original position, I waited impatiently.

As soon as we unloaded the cooking gear and my father started a fire, I approached my brother, Periclase.

"Hey, my dream ring is loose! That means you can have it now."

"Give that to me, peck." He ripped the ring from my outstretched hand and inspected it. I was glad, at the time, that he didn't inspect it too carefully. He didn't smell it, or he might have discovered my plan. I was about shaking out of my boots as he placed the small token on his finger. It seemed to shrink, sticking to the finger, holding tight.

"What're you grinnin' about, gobbo?" He brought his fist up and held it right in front of my nose. "It's mine now, meat-head."

I stayed awake almost all night, waiting with the orc repellent, ready to burst out of my blanket at any moment and throw it on my brother, reversing the effects of the potion that covered the ring.

I heard Periclase snore loudly. Looking over, I saw a smile form beneath his heavy mustache.

"Yes, smile," I whispered, "I'll show you who's a meat-head, Mr. Orcbait." I eventually fell asleep, the smile on my lips matching that on my brother's.

The next morning, I awoke to the smell of frying bacon, not the smell of orcs as I had expected. I opened my eyes to see my dad preparing breakfast. My eldest brother came up with a load of wood to add to the fire. I crawled to my feet and rubbed my eyes.

"Morning, Red," my dad greeted me. He always called me "Red" when he was happy. That meant he'd had a couple swigs of his "Mornin' Juice." He reserved my given name, Crimson, for when he was angry. That was most of the time. When he was really mad, he just called me "Boy."

"Mornin', Sir," I replied. I had to show the utmost respect to my dad, especially when he was in a good mood. It helped keep him there.

He offered me a cup of his strong root and mushroom tea. "It puts hair on your chest," he always said about the dark, bitter drink. So far, I hadn't noticed any hair on my chest, and certainly not enough on my chin.

Looking down at the mug as I accepted his offer, I noticed something glittery on his finger. Peering closer, I realized it was the ring of dreams that I had given to Periclase the night before.

"Wh–Where did you get tha–that ring?" I asked, trying to act as casual as I could, trying not to show the terror in my eyes.

"Peri gave it ta me. It's a dream-ring. He said it gave him a dream o' yer mum las' night." He stared past me at the far away mountains. "By my beard, I'd like ta see her again."

My hand was shaking as I took and drank the mug of tea. When my dad asked about it, I just said I was cold.

By noontime, I had almost forgotten about the orcbait. It must not be working, I convinced myself, feeling relieved. That relief was short-lived. Just before lunch, we heard thrashing in the underbrush.

"Into the wagon, Boy!" my dad shouted at me as he pulled me away from the campfire and threw me towards the caravan.

"Da! No! Don't go!" I feebly tried to stop him as he vaulted over the rocks, his axe already in his hand. He grabbed a flaming log from the fire to aid him in the fight.

The air was filled with shouting and growls. I ran back to the wagon to get my hatchet so I could help in the fray. I scrambled into the cart and started throwing open cases, forgetting where I had put it. I found it when I decided to search the first case a second time. It was buried beneath a sack of cornmeal.

I ripped off the blade protector and leapt from the cart, prepared, I thought, to kill anything that threatened my family. In my haste, I forgot the orc repellent.

When I returned to my father, the battle was almost over. Two orcs lay dead and my father and the merchants had surrounded the third. They taunted the beast, even though it towered over them. I could see that its dark green hide was ripped open in several places and its blood fell to the ground. I couldn't understand why the dwarves didn't just kill the monster outright, until I saw that one of the merchants was incanting spells, and his hands glowed with magical power. His magic had pinned the orc's right foot to the ground and weakened him so that he could do little harm to the dwarves. Still, the creature continued trying to attack my father, ignoring the others. Only I knew why.

A sharp pain in my back stole my breath and knocked me to the ground. Blinking the mud from my eyes, I struggled to get up. Something heavy held my chest to the ground and a thousand knives of pain stabbed into my back. I could not breathe and I could not pull myself even an inch off the ground. Shouts surrounded me, overpowered by the rumbling of the earth and the pounding of my heart. My life played before my eyes; then, the life of my family. Finally, the history of the world came to me, as told to me by my mother's father years ago.

The Brothers

"At first, it was just Mother Tyrra, and she was alone. Nay, not just alone, she was lonely, so lonely she cried and cried. Her tears covered her whole body and threatened to drown her. Looking down upon her, Father Sky took pity. He sent his four sons down to comfort her.

"The four sons dutifully took to their work. Brother Order designed the sun, the moon, and the stars to keep Tyrra company and to track the progression of the days, the months, and the years. Then, he tried to tell his brothers about his design, but they could not understand what he wanted of them.

"He tried again and again to tell them, but still they shook their heads. Finally, he crafted a song, for the brothers were all great musicians, and sang it to them. This song was the finest that ever he composed, filled with layer upon layer of harmony, and perfect in its symmetry and order, describing every detail of his design. At once, the brothers understood, and they started to craft the celestial bodies. Brother Order made the largest of the planets; that's why the elves call it by his name in their language: Yova. Brother Tyr crafted the red planet, the one closest to Tyrra. That's why we call it by his name, and the elves call it Mari, which is his name in their language. Brother Verdon crafted the next, which the elves call Veni, and Brother Defile made the innermost planet, Merkor. Finally, all four brothers got together and, with a little help from Father Sky, built the sun, the moon, and the stars.

"While they worked, they sang Brother Order's Song of the Stars. This cheered Tyrra and dried up her tears. Land began to show beneath the receding oceans on Tyrra. The brothers came down to her, wondering what more they could do to help her.

"Brother Tyr knew how to reshape bodies, make them more beautiful, and he thought it might cheer Tyrra to be beautiful. He created a plan for mountains and valleys, hills and plains, rivers and lakes and oceans. But when he told his brothers, they couldn't figure out all he was saying; it was too wondrous. So, he sat down and meditated. In his meditation, a song came to him, wondrously beautiful, grand and magnificent. He went to his brothers and sang this song for them, and instantly, they understood and began their work. Brother Defile split large chasms in the earth with his hammer. Brother Verdon smoothed out vast plains. Brother Order set the rivers in their courses, and Brother Tyr raised towering mountains. It was all very beautiful, as intricate and as wondrous as the song that they sang as they worked, Tyr's Song of the Earth.

"Still, the brothers sought more ways to help Tyrra. Brother Verdon sat down to devise a plan, and he designed creatures great and small, all connected together in a complex web of purpose, all working together for Tyrra. But when he told his brothers of his plan, they could not understand its intricacies. He tried and tried to explain, but to no avail. Finally, he devised a song, a song that included the grace of the trees and the subtlety of the moss, the thunder of the great wyrm and the soft step of the field mouse. When he sang his Song of Creation to the others, they immediately took up the tune and began creating. Brother Verdon crafted trees of all species. Brother Tyr made the animals that roam the earth. Brother Order created the birds and gave them wing. Finally, Brother Defile created the fungus and worms that recycle the waste of the other creatures.

"This entire time, Brother Defile was crafting his own plan. He plotted a dark plan of hatred and war between the creatures, of disease and death. Now he explained his plan to his brothers, but they could not understand the chaos that he described, so he began to sing. It began as a cacophonous sound, a dissonant and horrible, unmelodious tune. Then it began to grow until it echoed horribly through the forests and mountains and valleys, filling them with darkness. All the creatures, hearing the horrendous screech, began to run madly about. They convulsed and attacked each other. Disease began to spread through them.

"Defile's three brothers were horrified by what they saw, and wanted desperately to stop their brother's madness. They joined together, for Defile was stronger in power than any two of them, and only the three together could overpower him. With songs of joy and hope, they pushed back Brother Defile's Song of Pestilence and broke it into a thousand tiny echoes. But he began again with a new song, the Song of Devastation, which threatened to break apart the very body of Tyrra. This song caused earthquakes, landslides, storms, and tidal waves.

"The three brothers were deafened by this song and thought that they could not combat its power because it was too loud. Eventually, Brother Order had an idea, and he began singing a song that was similar to the Song of Devastation, so similar that Brother Tyr and Brother Verdon thought he had joined Brother Defile in the destruction of all that they had created. But soon, they heard a variation on the tune and now the song began to calm. Brother Order created melody out of cacophony, harmony out of dissonance. And when they heard what he was doing, Verdon and Tyr joined in, singing along with Brother Order in his Song of Calming. The song began to calm the storms, stop the shaking of the ground, and smooth out the seas.

"Brother Defile was starting to begin a new song, the Song of the Apocalypse, which was sure to destroy the whole of Tyrra and the celestial bodies, but his brothers had surrounded him and threatened him. At this time, Defile still wielded his Hammer of Unmaking, which was forged from the same steel as Brother Order's Hammer of Shaping. Fearing for his life, Brother Defile brought his hammer down and struck at the body of Tyrra. Where he struck, a great chasm opened, and the ground began to gush red. Mother Tyrra was bleeding from the wound.

"Everywhere a drop of her blood fell, however, something miraculous happened. A new kind of creature formed from Tyrra's life essence. These creatures were similar in shape to the four brothers, though much smaller, which caused the brothers to call them 'dwarves,' and the creatures to call the brothers 'giants.' These creatures had the stature of ordinary men, and they had beards that reached down and rooted them to the ground. They followed the will of Tyrra and marched against her aggressor. Though his hammer unmade thousands of them in a single stroke, their sheer numbers were too much for Brother Defile, and they were able to overpower him and drag him to the ground. With the help of the brothers, they tore apart his body, splitting it into seven pieces. The brothers then helped them hide the body parts beneath the mountains of the seven continents. The Hammer of Unmaking was swallowed up by the chasm that it had created.

"For many centuries, the three brothers worked alongside their newfound kin, rebuilding from the destruction caused by Defile's voice. The dwarves were good workers and knew how to heal Tyrra, having come from her essence. Each brother taught his arts to the dwarves, but no dwarf was ever able to learn all that the brothers could teach them. The brothers each wanted to teach all he knew to them, or even just to a small group of them. So, the three got together, and they decided to split the dwarves into three tribes. Then, each could teach his tribe the whole of his knowledge. However, they did not want to force any individual into a particular tribe, so they decided to allow each dwarf to choose his own path. They built a great chamber in the heart of Tyrra which they called the Nexus and invited the dwarves to come and choose their tribes. Each brother would have a chance to convince each dwarf to join his side. Thereby, no one brother would become unbalancingly strong by the addition of followers.

"The dwarves came down into the Nexus and each was offered a reward from the brothers. Brother Verdon offered great magic, keen eyes, and a kinship with nature. The people who chose him were called by him 'Aelfynkynd,' which meant 'People of the Trees.' They are the elves of today. Brother Tyr offered strength, numbers, and an unmatched fierceness, that his people might defend Tyrra from all future enemies. He called these people 'Umankynd,' or 'People of the Spear,' and they are called 'humans' today. Finally, Order offered courage and skill at crafting. The people who chose his path were called 'Tiokaikynd,' or 'People of the Anvil.' They were the ancestors of our people, the Tokai, who have inherited the name that was once the name of all people: 'dwarf.'

"But a number of people did not come to the Nexus. They protested that they did not want what the brothers had to offer. They did not want to serve the giants as slaves, they complained. The brothers did not know what to do, and the whole situation distressed Tyrra terribly.

She began to cry again. Remembering what had happened when her tears had covered her body before, the brothers went to their tribes. Each nominated one from each tribe to lead his people away from the floodwaters.

"The Aelfynkynd spoke to the trees, and the trees bent together and wrapped themselves around each other to form a huge vessel. The Umankynd felled trees and built a fleet of smaller ships. The Tiokaikynd, led by Prince Stoneheart, shaped the very earth into a mountainous boat. The other people had no leader and lacked the powers of the brothers to help them, so they were called 'Trulkynd,' which meant 'Lost People.'

"It was believed that the Lost People would indeed be lost in the threatened flood, but, as the waters soaked the ground, the earth turned to marsh. Brother Defile's spirit leaked out of his separated body and up through the black swamp. In the form of a serpent, he came to the Trulkynd and whispered foul words into their ears about the other brothers abandoning them and bringing the flood down upon them. He promised to help them seek revenge, if they would serve him. Defile's promises were sweet to hear, far sweeter than the promised doom offered by the flood, and most of the Trulkynd accepted. They took the appearance of the Dark Brother and his strength, along with an ability to heal quickly. This was Defile's plan that he imparted to them. He buried them deep within the earth, where the floodwaters could not harm them. When they receded, he would let them free again. But, in the forty years of flooding that followed, they began to despise the light. They hated it with so much passion that they would never look upon the sun again."

Ironfist Forge

I opened my right eye to see the sunlight filtering through the slats in the side of the wagon. I could not open my left. My head felt as if it had been hammered flat on an anvil. I tried to sit up, but the dizziness held me down. Turning to the side, I retched.

My brother, who was in the back of the wagon with me, leaned over with a towel to tend to my wounds. My flesh burned where the orc's massive claws had pierced it. The mixture on the towel smelled sweetly acrid, a combination of slippery elm and goldenseal, meant to stave off infection.

"Yer back's all cut up," Periclase said. He said it quietly, practically a whisper, but still the sound stabbed my brain. "I'm surprised you didn't take a trip to the Earth Circle. We don' know where the nearest one is, an' if you rezzed, we'd nae be able ta find you. Or perhaps yer spirit'd go all the way back ta Stonewood, and we'd have ta make the trip all over again."

The only response I could muster was a pitiful request for water.

He helped me drink some from a little wooden cup and continued, "The merchants cannae figure out why th'orcs attacked us. They're normally sleepin' around that time. We must've run into a hunting party or somethin'. Not large enough ta be one of those raidin' parties that've been mauradin' around this area. Perhaps a few stragglers at the end of the line. But, we've moved on in case they was scouts or some sort of advance group."

Having doused my throat a bit, I was able to form a few words, though in a low whisper. "How–how long?"

"How long was you out? About five hours. We gathered up the camp pretty quickly. We didn't even 'ave time to figure it out, you know? Like, why was they jus' goin' after Pa? The merchants still have no clue. The only time they ever saw somethin' like it was when Old Man Barkborer accidentally spilled some orcbait on 'isself."

At the sound of the word, I choked on the water. My brother didn't seem to notice, because he continued. "Anyway, we've kept to the main roads since then. The merchants decided they'd rather deal with bandits than orcs. An' if orcs attack, maybe the bandits'll turn out ta be on our side." This was long before the Kingdom of Evendarr settled the area, and there was little law outside of the towns. The only humans in the area preyed upon travelers, and caravans carrying the precious stonewood were their favorite.

"Are you feelin' strong enough ta eat?" Periclase asked, offering some flatbread.

Taking it, I ventured, "So, what dream did ya get from the ring?"

"About Mum," he replied. "Like nothin' ever happened. She was stirrin' a big pot o' stew an' tellin' me and Sis one of her stories. By Order's beard, I miss her." That was the first time, and the last, that I ever saw my brother cry. He didn't bawl, mind you, but his eyes watered up and a few brave tears escaped their jail to go running across the rutted landscape of his face.

I laid there for several hours, staring out the window at the rear of the wagon, grinding my teeth against the pain in my back, until we finally came to a stop.

My father burst through the door. His face was painted red with drink. "Boy!" he shouted at Periclase. "Go help yer brother tend the horses." He rarely called Peri "boy." He usually left that name for me. I shivered at the cold stare in his eyes, which was fixed directly at me.

"Crimson!" he shouted when my brother had scurried out from under the oppressive air which filled the wagon. "Yer gonna wish that orc 'ad killed you, because I'm nae gonna be as nice as 'im."

His arm flashed out with the speed and power of a man who had worked the forge for two hundred years. I heard my ribs crack beneath his hardened fist as I went tumbling to the floor. He knocked over the makeshift bed upon which I'd lain and pulled up the floorboards beneath.

"I knew t'was you, Crimson. When the others said they smelled orcbait, I thought it might be you. And when that dream ring smelled, I knew t'was you." He held up one of the bottles that I had pried the wax off. "You gave yer brother that ring. You tried to kill 'im! Now I'm gonna kill you!"

Blood half blinded the one eye I could open. Struggling to get to my feet beneath the flood of pain, I put my hand down on the small wooden box in which I had placed my treasure: the nymph's lily. I felt my father's tough hand grab hold of my shirt and haul me backwards. I swung around to meet him, and my arm flew out to meet his face. In slow motion, I watched his cheek crumple beneath the box. The box exploded into a thousand pieces, and the lily floated gently to the floor.

I managed to pick it up before my dad put his hands on me again. This time, he shoved me out the door and threw me to the ground. I tried to get up and run, but the pain in my back and legs held me down. A sharp pull on my hair, and my head snapped back. I felt something cold touch my throat.

"*With mystic force I build a prison!*" a new voice to my left shouted. I felt fire course through my body, and I stiffened. A glowing shell formed just outside my skin and clothing, then faded to invisibility. I could only move my eyes, not turn my head, so I couldn't see what was going on.

"Chilox!" a voice shouted. I recognized it as one of the stonewood merchants. "You better stop now. Come and sober up."

"He tried to kill us all! It's his fault... the orcs!" my father yelled.

"I don't care what he did! There's nothing that lets you break your own line! If he did something wrong, bring him before council, or at least the Grudgebearer."

"I should kill him now! It's what he deserves!"

"If you want him, you'll have to go through me."

"And me," a new voice added, my eldest brother's.

There was a tense moment before the hand holding the knife moved away from my neck. I couldn't feel it, just see the hand, my father's hand, lift slowly away, quivering. In fear or rage or drunkenness, I cannot guess. My brothers led my father away, I assume, because he was gone when the merchant dropped the spell that protected me.

"Are you alright, lad?" he asked, looking over the bruises my father had left.

"I–I will be." I could not look him in the eye for my shame.

It was several hours later when I saw my father again. He appeared more sober, but not much happier. He came to me that night around the fire. Once again, he drew his knife. My eyes grew wide with horror as he grabbed me by my short beard. Before I could wince, he brought the blade down and severed my already pitiful red whiskers. Where they had grown, new streams of blood dripped towards their source. One slice and I was branded as a liar and a fool. My dad stormed off, and I could only hang my head in shame. I knew that I deserved the death with which he'd threatened me. I knew that I deserved to be stricken from the Book of Records and have my line cut forever for betraying my family.

All of my wounds, including the one on my chin, had scabbed over and begun to form scars when we arrived in the Dwarfhaven Mountains several days later. Despite the rocky terrain, the road was rather smooth, because it was paved with limestone pulled from the heart of the mountains. It was obviously crafted by dwarves; no other race would have taken the time and care needed to make the road so precise and perfect. We rose up through several switchbacks and through Oakenshield Pass, where stand two great natural pillars of stone which rise high into the air to guard the entrance to Dwarfhaven: Tyrra's Fangs. Banded with every color of stone imaginable, from red to yellow to blue to white to grey and black, and jutting almost a hundred feet from their perches on either side of the pass, which were themselves eighty feet tall, the spires would have humbled even the most honored of dwarves.

Equally as stunning was the view that awaited us once we passed between the Fangs. Surrounded by the rocky peaks was a lush green valley. Rich pastureland was dotted with herds of sheep and goats. Springs from all sides formed streams that flowed down through wooded lanes down to a lake. Behind that lake, a sheer cliff wall towered up to the tallest peak in the range, Ironfist Mountain, and at the base of the cliff lay the entrance to Ironfist Forge, accessible only by way of a single bridge over the deep cold water. As we approached, I could see that part of the bridge could be withdrawn in the event of an attack and the great iron gates, which stood open, welcoming, could be slammed shut and barred, making the fortress almost impenetrable to its enemies.

I stared in awe as the caravan passed through the massive doorway into an incredibly tall cavern. Here, the lake followed us inside, and I realized that, if the need ever arose to close the outer gate, the lake would back up behind it as if behind a dam and the pressure would prevent anything from opening the doors.

The bridge was narrow here, and murder-holes could be seen along both sides of the cavern and in the ceiling. If an army managed to make it to this point, the soldiers would be magnets for arrows and hot oil. We felt hundreds of eyes watching us as the wagons wheeled over the underground river.

We approached a second set of gates, much smaller than the outer doorway, but made from the same thick steel. These, too, were opened, but guards stood by to check the waybills of every merchant that entered. Above the gates, a stern-looking statue of a dwarven king gazed down at us over his silvered beard. It was King Devin Stoneheart the Builder, founder of Ironfist Forge.

One of the guards looked over the waybills and checked the packages of those who went before us, but he just waved my father through. Dad knew everyone, because he did so much business all around the region. Either they did not suspect him of smuggling or they did not care.

The next chamber we entered was a huge marketplace. It was bustling with activity as traders from all around gathered to do business. Most of the deals were sealed through the use of Tradesign, a complex set of minute gestures and handshakes that would hide the details of the commerce from the uninitiated. All manner of things were bought and sold in this cavern, from livestock to jewelry to lumber to land, and people of all races traded here with the dwarves, but none of those outsiders would be allowed into the city proper, where we directed our wagons. The stonewood merchants did business with the king's own people and none of the product would be offered to the other races, though they would offer large sums for something as strong and versatile as stonewood.

We passed through a series of rooms that were not as large as the others, coming at last to a humongous cavern. The natural cave was so large that haze hid the far side from view. Giant buildings surrounded us, covering the bowl-shaped floor, and an incredibly tall tower stood in the center of the city. It was natural stone column, reaching all the way up to the misty ceiling. The thick fog that hung at the top of the cavern attested to its size; the cave was tall enough to have its own weather, and these were clouds that would periodically rain, forming the streams that flowed through the city and fed the underground river. The roar of the Redstone River echoed throughout the chamber, filling the whole city with its thunderous music.

We came at last to the pillar in the center of the city, and I could see that the river flowed around it, making it an island. We crossed over the drawbridge and my father gave the guard a nod. The wagon passed through a gate and arrived in a bright courtyard. Up until this point torches and small glowing stones had lighted our way, and it was far from being as bright as the surface above, but here, the whole place glowed as bright as noontime. Looking up, I saw that the center of the column, which we were now inside, was a solid quartz crystal that carried the sunlight belowground. Mirrors and faceted crystals all around the room split up the light and directed it around the chamber, making the courtyard bright enough for the many surface flowers and trees which were planted here to flourish.

My father reined in the horses at the foot of a crystal waterfall that sparkled with the brilliant reflected sunlight. He hopped down from the driving seat and gestured for my brothers to help him. They unloaded heavy barrels, which I knew were filled with father's wares, but which were labeled "Black Axe Breweries – Special Stonewood Stout."

A number of dwarves filed out of a passage to the left. I watched them intently, curious about their clothing. These were obviously people of importance. They wore long robes of various colors. The man in front of the group wore blue. Their beards were all long, white, and braided, and decorated with golden trinkets. They wore no hats, and the light shined off of their smooth, bald heads, but each wore a golden circlet, except for the leader, who wore a tall crown with sapphire jewels. His robe was decorated with golden runes.

As they came near, Periclase pried the lid off of one of the kegs. The man in blue reached inside and pulled out a beautiful shortsword. I did not know my father produced such magnificent work. It was etched with runes and magical symbols, and held a large emerald in its pommel. The dwarf swung it around, testing its weight and balance. He seemed pleased beneath his beard, but he quickly hid his grin when my father approached.

"Deal met," Dad said. "The drae wouldn't trade but for a hefty price. I had to give 'em double what you asked." That explained it; my father hadn't made these. They were traded from the dark elves, and were likely magically enhanced.

"Double!" the other dwarf exclaimed. "I thought you were a good bargainer. I thought you'd fetch it for half. In fact, I'll bet you did. You're pulling my beard, Chilox. Tell me the price."

"Like I said: double. Thirty thousand."

"You'll not be a gypsy, Chilox. Tell me the real price. I'll give you fifteen, as agreed."

"I paid twenty-five. I had to put it up front, too. They wouldn't give me credit, and I decided it wasn't wise to invoke your name, Majesty."

"True. True." The king reached back into the barrel and removed a silvery axe. "They are all stonewood?"

"Yes, Majesty, only the finest."

The dwarf admired the blade. "And the enchantments?"

"As you asked. I had them identified in Stonewood."

"Hmm. Discretely, I hope."

"Of course. One of my grandfather's line. As trustworthy as your beard is long, Your Majesty." The other dwarves watched in silence as my dad stared into the king's eyes. The king stared back, both becoming rocks. My father was stonewood, and the king backed down.

"Very well. Twenty-six."

"I need profit, Your Majesty. It cost more than a thousand to protect along the way. We were attacked by orcs." He threw a quick glance my way when he said that.

"I'm sorry, but twenty-six is all I'll do."

"Perhaps we can make a deal, Majesty, one that's not monetary."

"What's that?" the king inquired, his eyes twinkling at the possibility of coming out on top.

"My wife was killed by an orcish raiding party. I travel so much, my sons are often left without a guardian."

"They seem capable enough of guarding themselves," the king said, looking over my brothers, Periclase and Auric. He was right, their muscles showed beneath their tunics.

"It's not these two who have the problem. They travel with me. They're my apprentices. It's my youngest that needs looking after."

"And what do you want me to do? I have no need of new servants."

"No, Your Majesty. He has family in the valley, his mother's clan, Forgehammer."

"So, he can live with them! You don't need me. Make the arrangements with them."

My dad looked back at where I was huddled beneath a blanket, only my eyes disclosed. "He's not exactly desirable. He's as hardheaded as the forge's anvil, and he doesn't take easily to direction. I need you to be his advocate, to get the clan to adopt 'im."

"Hmm," the dwarf stroked his beard. "And what'll you do for me?"

"Twenty."

"That's still five over what I wanted."

"It's still a big loss for me," my father answered. After a silent moment of beard stroking, they shook hands and sealed the deal.

The Forgehammer Clan Council was planning to meet on a few nights later, so we stayed at an inn inside Ironfist Forge. Father and Auric spent their time and their gold down in the pub on the lower floor of the inn, laughing at jokes and telling stories to other travelers. Periclase and I were told to stay out of sight, and, not wanting to upset my father more than I had, I did so by wandering the streets of the city.

The underground domain held many new wonders for me. Everything, no matter how mundane, interested me. I watched with fascination as growers harvested mushrooms, jewelers set rubies, and brewers bottled ales.

On our third day in the city, I stumbled across something that really peaked my interest. In the upper reaches of this branch of the city, one of the crystal shafts that brings sunlight underground reaches all the way to the roof of a building. This intrigued me, and I sought a closer look.

The building at which it ended was old, covered with glowing moss. Its windows were dark and opaque. The rusty iron door, overhung with the same glowing moss, featured a giant brass knocker shaped like the head of a dragon. Above the door hung another brazen image of a dragon, this one decorated with stars.

I gave the door a hard shove, and it swung slowly open, noiselessly rotating on its hinges. It was dark inside; the crystal shaft did not illuminate the interior of the building. Only a few candles provided the light by which I could see the rows of shelves upon which sat all manner of trinkets and artifacts.

Looking around slowly, my eyes lighted upon bottles and books, scrolls and skulls. The store, as it appeared to be, was filled with every possible type of item, most decorated with arcane symbols. I saw wands, rings, crystals, medallions, and even a small doll. One particular item caught my eye. It was a crystal flower, a lily crafted of fine opal. I reached out to touch it, remembering the nymph who went by the same name as this fair flower. I could almost hear her voice calling my name... But what I could hear were the words uttered by a robed dwarf who had just entered the shop.

"Magick isn't something to be meddled with, young Crimson." I looked over to see the man. He was clothed in long dark blue robes that were decorated with runes and arcane symbols. Wrapped around his waist a few times, his beard was long and grey and braided with gold beard-rings.

"How–" I began, "how do you know–"

"Tut tut, a magician never reveals 'is secrets, little one." He smiled beneath his beard and gave me a little wink. "Now, that flower–a lily is it?–is quite a prize. She 'as some secrets of 'er own. But do ye 'ave enough gold to get it? I think the shopkeep is asking four fer that'n."

"No, sir, I only have one." My hand dropped down to a small pouch I wore on my belt, which contained the seven silver coins and thirty-two copper pieces I had saved over the past year. I had earned them doing small jobs for old widows in Stonewood.

"Well, I'm sure ye 'ave more'n that."

"No, sir, that's all I have."

Grinning, he reached his hand beneath my chin and withdrew it, three gold coins shining between his fingers.

"There they are. 'Iding them in yer beard, were ye?" he said as I looked at the coins amazed. "Now take yer lily an' run along. I'll settle the deal for ye."

Wide-eyed, I started to do as the old dwarf said.

"Oh, young Master Chilox!" he cried after me as I was stepping out the door. "The flower was four gold, and I only 'ave three."

"Oh! Right, sir." I reached down and undid the strap from the little pouch. Tossing it to him, I said, "Thank you, sir. I'll not forget it."

"Nay, me boy, ye won't. I'll not let ye."

That night, we waited for almost an hour while the clan deliberated on other matters. The meeting took place in a round stone amphitheater, built into a natural depression in the earth. Unlike most dwarven structures, it was open to the sky. A number of standing stones surrounded the circle, indicating by their wear that this place was far older than Ironfist Forge. Although its original purpose was unclear, it could still be used as a calendar. In fact, the Forgehammer Clan planned their meetings by the stones. This one had been called because the moon had risen directly over one of the stones. The circular stone floor of the amphitheater displayed many ancient arcane symbols. Around the floor stood the twelve clan elders, each perched on a different symbol, and each accompanied by a young boy holding a burning torch. In the center of the circle, the clan chief directed the meeting. The dwarves who were standing or sitting on the three tiers of the circle jeered when my father offered me for adoption.

"We don't want yer cast-offs, Stonewood," sneered one grizzled man, spitting as he spoke, his words echoed by hundreds of others.

"From what we heard," snarled another, "he's caused you an 'eap of trouble, an' yer lookin' to get rid o' him with clear conscience." All the while, I huddled beneath the blanket, hiding from the glares and shouts thrown my way.

My father raised his hand to hush the crowd. "Listen!" His gesture had little effect on the raucous crowd. "Listen! I give my word–"

"Your word is worthless, lowlander. Go climb a tree, elf-blood, half-breed!" This struck a nerve with my father, he wasn't proud of his line's choice of mates, and he had broken with his ancestors to choose a dwarven mistress. He drew his axe from the belt across his shoulder, and hefted the huge blade easily with one hand. Auric and Periclase drew their own weapons and moved to cover Dad's back, pushing me in between them. Under cover of the blanket, I pulled out my own small hatchet. I clutched the opal lily with my other hand.

With a growl, some of the nearest dwarves drew hammers, swords, and crossbows. Others began drawing energy from the earth, and their hands began to glow with a softly radiant green light. My dad muttered something about the king under his breath.

I felt anger well up inside me. I felt completely rejected. My father didn't want me; my mother's clan didn't want me; I was beginning to not want myself. My heart pounded. Fire burned behind my eyes. My head throbbed. A hoarse groan emanated from my throat. I heard a dark chanting, rising and falling, and knew that someone in the crowd was beginning the incantation of a spell. But it was not any of the common spells; it was in an ancient-sounding language that I had not heard before. It came in spurts, rising in volume and tempo, and then falling back to a slow, cold whisper. My skin began to glow black, if such a thing is possible. It seemed to suck in and absorb all light. I felt as if I were floating somewhere far off.

Once I noticed that I was the target of the spell, I looked around to find the source of the incantation. My brothers and my father had turned around to look at me, and the other dwarves also stared with seeming incredulity. None of the casters were speaking the incantation. In fact, they had all dropped their concentration and allowed the magickal energy they had drawn to fall back to Tyrra. It was then that I realized who was casting the spell. The strange words came from my own mouth.

I felt my body tremble with a shaking that grew more violent as the chanting increased in volume and pitch. My brothers backed away now, but I could barely see them through the haze that filled my vision. A multitude of voices whispered in my ears, drowning out the din of the crowd that now stood staring at me with wonderment and fear. I looked up at the night sky, and, to my amazement, I saw the sun. It shone down on me with a fierce light that burned my eyes and my skin. The moon moved across to eclipse the harsh orb. And when it had, I was bathed in a reddish glow. One voice became distinct from the others, thundering through my head:

"...and he shall be called by the color of blood, and through his blood shall the sun rise again, shining forth to guide all peoples on the path of enlightenment..."

The voice faded into the others once more, and, though I sought to follow it, I could not distinguish it from the others, which also began to fade. The moon slid back to its former position and the sun faded from my sight. The chanting slowed and stopped. My vision returned to normal, and I looked out at the faces of the crowd, my family having backed up and joined the other dwarves.

"What's all this?" asked a new voice, breaking the silence which now filled the gathering circle. The crowd parted to allow the king, accompanied by several guards, to approach the center, where I now stood alone. Hardly anyone took his eyes from me, and no one bowed until I did, my forehead almost touching the stone floor. The king turned around and raised his hands, oblivious to the fearful looks, which were still turned my way. "Now, now. There shouldn't be any arguing over this boy. I offer my own personal advocacy of the boy's lineage, and ask you, as his kin, to take him in as one born to your daughters. I know—"

"I will take 'im as me apprentice," a gruff voice called from the far end of the amphitheater. The crowd parted again, revealing an ancient dwarf in long dark blue robes embellished with runes and symbols that mirrored those of the amphitheater floor, the same dwarf whom I had met in the magick shop.

The king gave a slight laugh. "But, Guildmaster, he has not yet been tested. He is not ready to become an apprentice, especially not to one as skillful and knowledgeable as yourself. Surely, you do not wish to waste your time training a boy who may have no aptitude for the," he gave a slight frown and added an odd emphasis to the next word, as if it left a bad taste in his mouth, "magickal arts."

"I doubt that anyone who witnessed the boy's," the guildmaster paused as if choosing his words carefully, "demonstration would believe I was wasting my time."

The king looked around in astonishment, for he had not seen the event that prompted the guildmaster's interest.

"Well, surely *you* don't mean to adopt the boy and raise him as your own!"

The wizard shook his head. "No, ye know 'ow my apprenticeships work. 'e will be adopted by another and learn a—"

"A valuable trade?" The king was obviously trying to anger the other dwarf, who continued as if he was never interrupted.

"–trade that will allow 'im to support 'isself while 'e learns the rudiments of the mystical arts."

"Well, you don't know any of those, so I guess you won't be taking the boy in."

"The boy will learn to craft armor from 'is grandfather."

"And where is he then?" the king asked heatedly. "I see no grandfather here."

The mage slowly lifted his arm to point up towards the highest level of the amphitheater where a few dwarves still sat. People scurried like rats to remove themselves from the potentially dangerous path of magic, but the man's hand was not glowing; he was simply pointing. At the rim of the bowl, next to one of the standing stones, an ancient dwarf looked down on the proceedings from a chair he had crafted himself, a chair that allowed him to move under his own power, even though his legs had long ago been shattered. My grandfather nodded slowly.

"Very well, then. I see you have everything worked out," the king finally said with a scowl, and, turning briskly on his heels, he strode from the circle. His guards followed, and not without a few wary glances back at the magician, who began to address the crowd.

"'ear me out! This boy will be as a son to all of ye. Inside of 'im dwells a great power, and 'tis growing in strength. As 'tis me responsibility to nuture and train this power, so 'tis yer duty to comfort and teach the dwarf in which it resides. Ye 'ave all witnessed a testament of this inner power, but be warned that mine own power is far greater, and if anyone mistreats the young one, 'e will 'ave to answer ta me.

"Though 'e wants ta be free of it, 'e will keep the name Crimson, for it will serve 'im as a reminder of the Right Way. When 'e 'as freed 'isself from the fate that the name warns of, 'e will free 'isself from the name, but 'e will never drop the name entirely, for it must remind 'im of the blood that 'as been shed."

Crimson

In the year 394, Evendarr Reckoning, just over two hundred years ago at the time of this writing, and little more than a hundred years before my father brought me to Ironfist Forge, the capitol of the dwarven kingdom of Validor was destroyed. The city of Trollsgate had stood for generations, and many brave soldiers had lost their lives defending her from the dreaded Trullkynd, but Bradock Bouldershoulder, son of the chieftan of Clan Bouldershoulder, fell asleep at his post. His snoring, survivors of the resulting massacre say, was so loud that it covered even the heavy footsteps of the trolls as they entered the city.

Clan Bouldershoulder now lives in disgrace. The clan has produced many great adventurers, each seeking to restore honor to his clan, and many of these adventurers have given their lives in that quest. The once bountiful clan now numbers less than fifty individuals.

Under the guidance of his advisors, King Kelanor II decided to abandon Trollsgate and move his capitol to the fortress city of Dwarvenholm. One of these advisors was Bulk Adamas, a general in the dwarven army and friend of Kelanor. Bulk assured Kelanor that they would one day return to his beloved Trollsgate, but that survival was of utmost importance. By regrouping in Dwarvenholm, they could amass a far larger offensive to drive the trolls back out of the city. The other advisors were guildsmen and knew little of military strategy–nor did Kelanor; they simply wanted to move their wealth as far from the rampaging trolls as possible.

The city of Dwarvenholm was much easier to defend. It was built by the finest dwarven architects of all time, and designed to be perfectly defensible. The kingdom began to recover from the destruction of the old capitol, but the guilds wanted to expand faster. They urged Kelanor to allow them to expand the city above ground, to create an open city that could become a center for trade with the other races.

Bulk, like many of the soldiers, was wary of creating such relationships with the other races. He grew up with tales of the Baracoor and of the treachery of the elves, and was filled with a deep distrust of non-dwarven peoples. He urged Kelanor not to compromise

Dwarvenholm's security with the building of the open city. What kept the dwarven riches safe, he proclaimed, was the fact that only dwarves knew where the city was or how to get to it.

Against Bulk's urging, Kelanor ordered the construction of the open city. The argument which followed between the two dwarves is recorded in the *Annals of the Dwarvenholm Great Moot, Volume MCCLXIV: Records Pertaining to the Investigation into the Death of His Majesty King Kelanor II Stoneheart of Validor, Lord of Trollsgate and of Dwarvenholm.*

"You'll regret this, Sire," began Bulk, "Trolls will swarm all over here. The barbarians will pillage the open city. Elves will—"

"Elves will trade with us, and pay a fine price for dwarven steel."

"And whom do you think that steel will be used against, Your Majesty. Didn't you grow up with the same horrid tales of the Elf War that I did?"

"Myths, my dear Bulk," the king replied. "Old stories told to teach us lessons."

"Well," the soldier raised his voice angrily, "You haven't learned their lessons, obviously. Aelfynkynd betrayed us once; they'll do it again! And you can't possibly trust the humans. They've always been the People of the Spear. They even turn their spears against one another for gold, and it won't be long before they turn their spears against you for yours."

Bulk continued, "If you build this open city, I will leave, and many dwarves will follow me."

"Words of treason, Sire!" One of the other advisors, Corin Gemcrusher, Master Merchant, stood up to shout his accusation across the hall.

"Silence, you greedy bastard!" The king's angry response sent him back into his chair. "You've threatened worse. Why is it treasonous from his mouth, but not yours?"

He turned back to his old friend. "Do not go, Adamas. I disagree with you on this. The open city will bring great wealth into dwarven hands, and it is the only way to recover from the fall of Trollsgate. We must amass great wealth to return and push the enemy from our lands.

That is why a tax shall be levied on all goods traded in the open city." The guildsmen gasped at this revelation and murmured quietly to each other. "The army shall benefit from the greed of our merchants."

After stealing an angry glance at Gemcrusher, Kelanor continued, "Your advice, Bulk, has been indispensible to me thus far."

"Then why won't you listen to it now?"

"Though I disagree with you now, I have never stopped listening. Stay, and respect that I have thought the matter over, considering every angle, and I have decided to build the open city. Your strategic mind will be needed to defend the open city from the very threats which you have to me described."

After that, Bulk Adamas was named Grand Vizier to His Majesty Kelanor II. He was presented with a magickal hammer forged by Guildmaster Ulin himself. Representative of Bulk's pledge to defend Dwarvenholm against all her outside enemies, the hammer could cause vast amounts of damage, but only to creatures not of dwarven stock.

Bulk oversaw the construction of the open city, and redirected its designs to make it the most easily defended aboveground city in the world, but it was still weak in comparison to the Dwarvenholm fortress city of old. He faithfully defended his vow to protect the city from outside enemies, but he could not know that the worst enemy the kingdom would face was already within.

In 433 E.R., one year after construction on the open city was completed, King Kelanor II died when a building collapsed around him. Foul play was suspected and an investigation was launched. The guildsmen tried to pin the treasonous act on Bulk Adamas, but no such connection was ever accepted by the Great Moot. Bulk contended that the guilds were the guilty party, but he was not successful in arguing his claims either.

Kelanor had one son, also named Kelanor, who was now crowned as King Kelanor III of Validor, but he was only a beardless boy, just eight years old. Much to the chagrin of Bulk Adamas, Vashta Stoneheart was appointed regent, and acted with the full authority of the crown. It was known that the guilds had their hands in his coffers, and he only acted for their interests. Over the next few years, the throne lost much of its former power and glory, and new privileges were extended to the guilds. The Council of Masters, an assembly of the Guildmasters of every major guild, became the true ruling authority in Dwarvenholm.

Bulk was removed from his post and stripped of his rank. Nothing more is recorded of him for ten more years.

The dwarven wealth did indeed grow with the increased trade brought to Dwarvenholm by the open city. Unfortunately, Kelanor's vision was not put into practice. The guilds did not want to pay any more taxes than they already did, and the army never received these much-needed funds. The streets of the open city became dangerous. Bandits would wander through, easily taking dwarven gold for themselves.

A group of dwarves, calling themselves the "Crimson Militia," began to take the matter into their own hands. They killed any outsider who caused a serious threat. Their leader, wielding a fiercely glowing hammer, was Bulk Adamas.

Instead of returning the recovered wealth to its owners, however, the Crimson Militia kept it for themselves, calling it "collecting taxes." They began to prey on weaker groups of outside merchants, stealing their wares and gold.

"If it ain't got a beard, it'd better be afeared," became the motto of the Crimson Militia, and the outside merchants were indeed scared. Lesser merchants began to stay away, and those with more money, and more greed for dwarven steel, armed their escorts heavily.

But the Crimson Militia grew in number. The army, pushed by the guilds, tried to seek them out, but many of the soldiers were also militia members, and the search was only half-hearted. The army was asked to provide armed escorts for visiting merchants, but Bulk knew who would be loyal to him, and many times the defending dwarves would turn against their protectees and join the militia, never to be seen again.

Eventually, the Crimson Militia began to raid nearby settlements and merchant camps. Trading parties began to stay away. Rumors began to spread that the dwarves could not keep control of their own people.

One human, Fador Neuvin knew of a way to protect his merchants from the attacks of the Crimson Militia. With powerful magick, he turned all of his people into dwarves. The looked exactly like dwarves, right down to the tips of their beards, and they sounded exactly like dwarves. Bulk Adamas believed that they were dwarves from another nation, and allowed, nay welcomed, them into Dwarvenholm.

"'Bout time they got enough sense to trade with dwarves," he was heard saying as the Crimson Militia celebrated the news with several stolen barrels of elven wine.

Bulk went to meet the newcomers, who had been cleverly coached in the history of Arvain, a dwarven kingdom across the sea. He and his men excused any human mannerisms as characteristics of the dwarves on that far-away continent.

It was here, the old ones say, that Bulk first laid eyes on Fiona Baldalor, the woman that he would come to love. Corin Gemcrusher saw Bulk's advances towards the human woman who had been transformed into a dwarf. He immediately went to meet with Fador Neuvin and formed a plan to bring about the downfall of the thorn that had caused such a pain in his side.

They paid Baldalor to seduce Bulk, and their plan worked wonderfully. Under her influence, he put up his hammer and stopped feuding with the guildsmen. The Crimson Militia, left leaderless, began to fall apart. They no longer were as successful in raiding the merchant parties. It looked like everything was going to go smoothly, like Bulk was finally out of the guilds' beards.

One night, however, Bulk awoke to hear voices in the adjoining room. Fiona was not at his side, as she had been when he fell asleep. Her voice was one of those that he heard. The other was Corin Gemcrusher. Bulk snuck quietly to the door to hear better.

"The fool does nae suspect at'all." Fiona's sweet voice was tarnished with an angry huskiness. "How much longer must I keep this charade?"

"Ye'll keep it as long as we pay ye."

"Then ye'll 'ave tae pay me more. I did nae plan on being a dwarf's lover when I signed up tae work for Neuvin."

"Ye should consider y'self honored to be chosen for that role," Corin haughtily replied.

"Raise my wages," Fiona quickly shot back, "or I'll leave tonight."

"Do not worry, my sweet. 'Twill not be much longer. We're going to kill him soon."

"I could kill him tonight in his sleep."

"And be hanged tomorrow," the merchant told her. "We need it to look like an accident. Everything is in place, but things must wait a few days before moving forward. Ye must be patient, darling."

"I'm not your darling, anymore than I'm his."

"Hmmph. I thought yer new dwarven body would 'ave taught ye new darven manners!"

Bulk's eyes exploded with surprise. He was used to backstabbing and double-crossing. The fact that his beloved did not love him was no great blow, but that she was not even a dwarf—that twisted his insides into a solid piece of anger.

Moments later, he burst through the door into the outer chamber. His hammer was in his hand, glowing with fiery death. He struck at Fiona first, and she collapsed almost immediately. He brought his hammer back and hit Gemcrusher, but his blow was ineffective. Instead of hurting the merchant, the hammer flared up and burned Bulk's hand. He dropped it in surprise as the guildsman fled out the door.

Bulk turned back to Fiona's body, and tears began to form in his eyes. But it was not her death that destroyed the man's spirit, but her final words.

With a sudden gasp of breath, Fiona opened her eyes. Her voice was barely a whisper, and Bulk had to lean over to hear it.

"This is my final death, the spirits tell me. And so, I must tell ye now. I truly loved ye. I was still working with 'em so I'd learn how ye were to die, and I'd save ye. But now that plan won't work. I really did love ye, Adamas."

At first he believed it, and he wailed because he had lost his love, but soon doubt crept into his heart, and hatred began to build. He turned once more to the Crimson Militia, and their numbers grew even larger, to include a thousand dwarves. The changed their name now, from the Crimson Militia to Clan Crimson, and named Bulk Adamas, now Bulk Crimson, chieftain of their clan.

Trade slowed down to a crawl, but the guilds had a new plan. In 452 E.R., they made a deal with the human Kingdom of Evendarr. They signed a treaty that nominally put Evendarr in control of Dwarvenholm. The humans did not know of the undercity, the main part of Dwarvenholm that existed underground, and so believed there to be only around three hundred dwarves living in the city. Still, they proved to be a mighty nation, and Clan Crimson was no match for their soldiers.

Bulk led his clan to a remote location in the Forsaken Hills, and from there, they have continued to speak out and fight out against that which they call the "de-dwarving" of Dwarvenholm.

Apprenticeship

For many years, I worked solely as my grandfather's apprentice. Finally, I was allowed to enter the forge, but not as I had dreamed. I was not allowed to work the metal. My main job was to gather coal from the stone storehouse and cart it in a wheelbarrow up the steep rocky path to where my grandfather worked in the forge. Then I had to shovel the heavy loads into the furnace and pump the bellows.

"Move faster," my grandfather always shouted at me over the roar of the flames. "The fire won't get hot enough unless you pump it faster. I need the metal tae glow white hot. It's barely red and taking forever to get there. And you need tae move quicker getting the coal here, too. The fire almost dies in the time it takes you now."

"That's all the better I can do," I'd retort between heavy breaths. "It's tough. The coal is heavy and the bellows takes all my weight and strength." My arms strained with the effort of pushing down the long handle and hauling it back up. My grand wheeled around in his chair and took the handle in just one hand. He pushed it down with seemingly no effort and pulled it back up far quicker than I had managed. His arms didn't seem to strain at all with the work that had given me so much trouble. After a few pumps, the fire flared up white, and he returned to the anvil.

"Go and fill the buckets with water, boy, for the basin. And bring back a pitcher from the springhouse for me. Quickly now, boy."

"Yes, sir." My words were drowned by the loud, even ring of his hammer as he shaped a breastplate. The same even tones followed my further up the hill to the pumphouse.

When my grandfather worked with leather, it was my job to carry the heavy hide to his shop and to thread the long curved needles he used. Sometimes, I had to thread the feeds on the press he used for thicker leather. When he was crafting chain mail, I helped him melt the steel into the wire he then spun into tiny rings. But usually, he made plate, and I had to keep the furnace fueled and hot. I became stronger, and soon I was able to pump the bellows fast enough to keep the fire white hot.

A few times, the wizard came to speak with my grandfather, but he always sent me off on some errand, and I was never able to eavesdrop on their conversations. I assumed they were talking about me and my apprenticeship. I wondered when I was going to begin working for the mage. It had been several months and I had not heard a word about it. Always when I got back from my errand, the guildmaster was gone, and my grandfather put me right back to work.

In my limited spare time, mostly at night, I practiced making chainmail with the rings that had failed my grandfather's careful inspection and some old tools I had found in the store shed. I would examine his work and try to replicate his methods, but my simple projects usually fell apart before they became very large or twisted together instead of forming the neat rows and hexes my grandfather crafted.

One day when the master came, I stayed behind to hear what he had to say to my grandfather. I knew they would flay me if he found out, but I couldn't resist the chance to find out what they said about me. I had tried already to do this several times, but I had never correctly anticipated the errand that would be his excuse.

This time, he finally sent me to fetch water from the spring. I lowered my face to hide my joy as I thought about the jugs I had hidden behind the house. Rushing from the room, I snuck to my spot beneath the window, where I could hear every word.

"He's not ready." The gruff voice of my grandfather came drifting through the glass.

"Hasn't he grown stronger?" the guildmaster asked. I looked down at my arms, now bulging with the muscles I had gained by hauling coal.

"Yes," my grandfather replied, "but his strength is physical, not mental. He still has not the discipline your art requires, nor mine art."

"Hrm... He's still as stubborn as his lowland father?" I clenched my fist. How dare he use 'lowland' as if it were an insult?

"Well, he's arrogant, likely also from his father's side. My family has always been humble, obedient, but he knows he's getting strong; he wants more strength without work. He thinks he can become powerful without learning the basics. He's been working the metal in his room at night. Chain! He's been working on chain, and I haven't even taught him leather yet." I gasped. How did he know I had been working beyond my learning? "He doesn't have the patience to see things through to the end in the proper way; he's always got to jump ahead."

The guildmaster sighed. "I'm afraid he will always want the quick way. When he gets older, he'll make a decision to get power quickly. 'E won't know at the time that that path will take him much longer in the end."

And what did that mean? I was ambitious, not arrogant! There is nothing wrong with a little ambition; no man became great without it. I deserved to learn more than he was teaching. I was smarter than he gave me credit for. He was holding so much back from me. It wasn't fair. He wanted me to be his apprentice forever! He didn't want me to ever learn the magickal arts for which I was destined.

"He's got a strange destiny, a connection with powerful forces," continued Guildmaster Feldspar.

What was he implying? I was not possessed. I'd show him. I was going to be the most powerful wizard on Tyrra, with or without his help.

With the rage welling up inside me, I went to grab the pails of water that I had stored away for the occasion. When I presented them to my grandfather, now finished talking with his guest, I could only assume he attributed my anger to being sent away. I slunk away, not saying anything lest my words betray my heart. Damn him and his backwards ways that prevented me from being an armorsmith and a magus.

That night, I worked extra long at my experimentation with the rings. It was so frustrating. They wouldn't stay in the pattern. No matter what I did, they fell apart. I cursed loudly, wishing they would just burn and take my grandfather and the mage-master with him.

I grabbed the crystal flower from its perch on my small desk. I always held it when I was upset. The sorcerer had been right; it did have some magick to it. It calmed my rage when I looked at its graceful, softly glowing petals. This time, however, my anger was too great even for its power. I cursed again. I hated them both and wished they'd disappear.

What happened next astounded me. The rings began to glow, heating up. I dropped them quickly, and they began to shrink. Flames burst around them. Soon, there was nothing left of them. I checked, but the floor was not burnt where they had lain.

I began to cry and clutched to lily tighter. Surely, this meant that I was possessed. What was I to do? I was a danger to my grandfather and to everyone around me. I was sure that there was only one solution, to run away. But I knew nothing about the world, nothing that would help me survive in the wilderness. I did not even know a trade, which would help me survive in a far off civilization. The flower shattered when I threw it against the wall.

I took to learning armorsmithing with a new fervor. I chose not to complain about the work my grandfather had for me. I was the best apprentice I could be, sure that he would open up and share his trade with me, and he began to teach me all of his secrets. I picked it all up pretty quickly. We blazed through leather. This was no surprise; I had watched him make more leather than anything else, and there was only a little technique to making a good piece of armor. Then he taught me chainmail. I took to this eagerly, knowing that this type of armor would set me free. It took me a few years to learn to make a strong chain shirt, but I kept patient, as generations upon generations of my ancestors had done before me.

I began to love the metal. It spoke to me; its power resounded in my arms and kept me in my grandfather's forge. In my thirty-fifth summer, my grandfather taught me about plate mail, and I was never happier. I forgot about the magus and his empty promises. I forgot about infernal possession and strange happenings, and I forgot about running away. This was especially easy because I had not seen the master sorcerer in all this time.

After I was named a journeyman smith, the Forgehammer Clan truly accepted me as one of them. They, too, forgot about the events which had brought me here and the strange events that had happened at the council meeting. No longer did the rumors fly at my passing. I no longer dreamed each night of my father returning to take me back to Stonewood. My mother's death seemed so far away.

Finally, the day came that I was ready to start learning my trade by working at my own forge. My grandfather proudly presented me with a small anvil, suitable for working while traveling, and helped me build a traveling workshop from an old wagon. He handed me a pouch of coins.

"During a craftsman's apprenticeship, his master holds all of his earnings, so that he won't squander them," he said, pressing the bag into my hand. "I have received this money in payment for the armor which you made. It's your gold. Buy what supplies you need."

I spent a week gathering up the provisions I would need to spend a year on the road, crafting armor. I bought steel and leather. I made new tools at my grandfather's forge. I needed to get food, travel clothes, and other things to support me on the way to the next town, where I could sell armor for more supplies.

I would be traveling with other merchants for a while, many of whom had armed escorts or knew how to fight, so I wasn't worried about defense. Besides, I had my heavy hammer, and we dwarves had a saying: "Look to the left of your tools." Any tool, be it a woodcutter's axe, a haybaler's fork, a miner's pick, or a mason's trowel, could be used as a weapon. My hammer would suffice if we were attacked, and I would repair and maintain the armor of our party.

While I was in Ironfist Forge gathering my supplies, I found myself in front of the store in which I had met the mage who had shown such interest in me. It had been a long time since I had even thought about him, and I thought it strange that I had not seen him since that night that the chain links had disappeared. Hadn't he wanted me to be his apprentice? Now, I was headed away from the mountains as a journeyman in another guild. I guessed I would never see the longbeard again.

I slowly opened the door to the shop, partly wishing I'd find his smiling face waiting on the other side. The inside was very much the same as it head been last time I was there. Little had changed, except for the addition of a new layer of dust over the books, wands, and knick-knacks.

After looking around the shop for a few minutes, I turned to leave, but before I got to the door, something caught my eye. It was a small white object that glowed faintly. Upon close inspection, it appeared to be a flower, a lily, crafted of fine opal, just like the one I had destroyed, except that this one was closed like a bud.

I picked it up and rolled it between my fingers. The tingle that I felt was the same as the one that I had felt from the other flower. I placed it in the palm of my hand to examine it closely.

The glow became brighter. The petals began to turn and open. It took its final form, identical to that of the original flower, and a small piece of parchment fell from inside. I could not read at the time, so I shoved the paper into my pouch and made my way to the shopkeep's desk.

His desk was covered with papers and books, and he was carefully scribing some figures from a book onto a scroll. He had completely finished the page before he looked up to see me.

"I've never seen anything like it," he said after inspecting the opal lily. "I can't figure out what its properties are. How much are you looking to get for it?"

"No, no," I replied. "I'm not selling it. I just picked it up off your shelf. I'd like to buy it."

"Nonsense. I've never sold a crystal flower before." This statement surprised me. What about the one I had gotten from here many years ago?

"You sold its twin almost twenty-five years ago."

"No, no. Never seen anything like it before," the storeowner insisted. "Run along now. I don't have patience for nonsense and jokes."

I left the store feeling puzzled. Surely the dwarf had been mistaken. I had gotten the other lily from this very shop, and this one was sitting on his shelf, covered with dust, just like all the rest of his wares. I wouldn't have noticed it if it hadn't glowed.

I slipped the flower into my pouch. Suddenly, I remembered the parchment. I pulled it out and went to look for a scribe who'd be willing to interpret it for a few coins.

"Crimson, you will become a great mage without me, and you will bring the sun to burn away the shadows. Today, I bequeath to you my name. Wear it well. –Guildmaster Feldspar Sunlev'gantano" Every one of the four readers I hired said the same thing. I was sure that the first had been playing a joke on me, somehow getting wind of my situation, but when four scribes, in different parts of the city, said the same thing, word for word, I was forced to believe its validity.

I bought a small protective box for the flower. A few days later, I was on the road. I traveled mainly with a weaponsmith who was a cousin of mine, Josef Forgehammer. He was about twice my age and had traveled this way many times. From him, I learned how to wield bladed weapons, including swords, axes, and short spears. I was never extremely good at it, but I could hold my own in a fight.

When I returned to Ironfist Forge a year later, my grandfather had died when a particularly bad winter storm had collapsed the house around him. I spent a few weeks with family before I set out again.

I traveled through many towns and spent many years crafting and selling armor. I was one hundred fourteen before I saw once again the colorful stone trees of the Stonewood Forest.

Stonewood

Ah, to outlive our peers, to form a mighty empire that lasts for generations beneath our rule, to outlast infinity. We all dream these impossible dreams. Whole nations are created or destroyed in quest of these hopes. Stonewood itself was shaped by one dwarf's dream of immortality, and of love.

It was a time when the mountains were young. Ringold Oakenstone, son of the mighty King Barinold Lodestone, gained recognition during the dark battles with the gorgons in the Deeps. Ringold's leadership allowed the dwarves to find victory. He excelled in the art of magic and wove intricate and cunning spells that deceived and ultimately defeated their enemy. Barinold left the throne of his Lodestone Mountain Kingdom to Ringold, who he believed would be wise to assume power during this time of recognition and goodwill.

As the years passed, King Ringold carved a mighty fortress city beneath the mountains that once rose from the western forests of what is today the Duchy of Elysia. His people explored the realm, opening hall after hall of spectacular treasures and reaping wealth in jewels and minerals to glorify the kingdom. King Ringold spent much of his time perfecting his magic and traveling to remote areas of his kingdom in search of magical components that could lend power to his enchantments. It was in his 125th year that the king had a fateful meeting as he was passing through the Horningwood Forest.

Following his evening meal, Ringold decided to rest beneath a magnificent oak. It was one of the tallest trees in the forest, and by far the most beautiful. As he sat listening to the chirrup of insects and watching the lengthening shadows as the sun continued its long march across the sky, the king's ears caught a faint tinkling, and he noticed a ripple of light which emanated from the tree itself. Ringold found himself adrift on an ocean of light in which each silent whisper of the wind in the branches created turbulent shadows that fluttered and sparkled in his eyes.

As the daylight continued to fade, King Ringold saw a small movement in the woods ahead. He heard the tintinnabulation once more, and the movement came closer.

Breaking loose from the spell, he jumped to his feet and called out, "Who goes?"

Silence.

He waited, scarcely breathing.

Still nothing.

Then, another tiny movement to his left. He willed himself to remain perfectly still. A tall, slender figure emerged cautiously from the brush and slowly approached him.

King Ringold Oakenstone felt his breath escape his lungs as he beheld the dryad Nephtali Nirealis, queen of her people. He stood between her and the tree of her bondage, the home to which she must return each evening at the time of the setting sun. Her skin was as flawless as the petal of a rose in the first blush of its opening. Her silken hair reflected the color of the oak and glowed with strange green lights that danced and shimmered as she moved.

She approached with the grace of a young sapling swaying in the light breeze of a warm spring day. Ringold, overcome by her beauty and afraid she would disappear, stepped forward to intercept her and she stopped, just short of the oak. Her need for the tree overcame her fear of him, and she started to leap for a low branch. Ringold sprang into the gap and caught her in his arms. She cried out in terror, and he loosened his grip, smiling to assuage her fear. He placed her gently onto the limb, then, still holding her in his arms, he spoke for the first time.

It is not known what words passed between them there, or how Ringold was able to express the love he felt. Perhaps it was his magical power, his influence over the planes that attracted this creature of the earthen plane, or perhaps his studies had made him such an eloquent wordsmith that his poetry drew her heart to him. All that can be known with certainty is that Nephtali returned his love with the same passion that he gave it.

King Ringold tarried in the forest for a time, but he knew that he must soon return to his duties and his people. He was saddened and angered by the cruel whimsy of fate that bound him to this creature of nature who was bound to the oak forest and whose life was as fleeting as the breath of spring. He was a dwarf, with a lifespan easily six times her own, and able to move the lengths of Tyrra freely.

Eventually, he and Nephtali separated, and he returned to his mountain kingdom. Once there, he applied himself to the study of Earth and Celestial Magic with an intense obsession. He struggled with arcane arts and terrible elemental forces, seeking to tame and blend the tides that flow between the elements of stone, lightning, fire, and ice.

Finally, in the dark of his mountain stronghold he invoked a terrible magic that shook the entire kingdom. The mountains cleft asunder around him and spewed forth molten ash in a monstrous roar. The Elemental Plane of Stone was skewed and teetered in an unstable equilibrium, gobbling small pockets of other elements until it collapsed edgewise into the Horningwood Forest. King Ringold, stumbling from the ruins of his mountain, wandered as one lost, his mind enfeebled and broken by the powerful energies with which he had wrestled.

Nephtali found him lying near a brook in the forest and slowly nursed him back to health. As he regained his senses, he looked with shock upon the world that he had created. The blending of planes had caused the trees to take on an aspect of stone, so very hard that they defied even the sharpest of blades. The dryads joined to such trees were no longer mortal. The passage of their lives became to them as a living dream. The river of time bent in upon itself at the vortex of this curvature of planes, and they became a sequence of images fashioned upon its surface, forever caught in its sphere. Yet, viewed from the present, at any particular moment, they appear no different to mortal folk, and Nephtali appeared so to Ringold.

Thus was his love bought at a dear price. His kingdom was in ruins. His people were destroyed or scattered. The forest was irreparably changed.

Ringold and Nephtali vowed to rebuild a kingdom in the stone halls of the Horningwood Forest, and such a kingdom the likes of which this world may never see again. Many tales are told of this joining of dwarf and dryad and the magic they wove. Although the line of Ringold and Nephtali has slowly dwindled, it is still said that it cannot fail as long as the Stonewood Forest stands and Nephtali's tree remains unharmed. Thus, no dwarf to this day will take down a tree belonging to a dryad.

House Silversword

As I traveled along the road to Stonewood, my heart leapt in my chest. Memories of my old home poured into my head. I looked at every tree, hoping to glimpse a dryad. Once or twice I thought I saw one, but when I blinked she was gone. The road was paved with shavings from the stonewood forges, worn smooth by the passage of thousands of caravans. Myriads of colors glittered up from its surface. I urged the yaks that pulled my wagon forward. They were slow, lumbering animals, but they could handle carting a smiths workshop through snowy mountain passes far better than could horses. Right now, they were much too slow for my liking.

I looked around with wonderment. The merchants and adventurers with whom I traveled were all business. There stone facades did not betray any hidden interest. They had all seen the sights of Stonewood many times, and any special luster it may have once held had long since faded away. I wondered if the situation might be opposite in the grand halls of Ironfist Forge.

The fortress wall that once stood around the entire town showed huge gaps where the timbers had been carted away. After the armies of Evendarr had destroyed most of the antagonistic orc tribes in the War of the Bloody Fist, the townspeople's greed had overpowered their need of protection.

I met my brethren in the tavern in Stonewood that night. Every Stonewood dwarf wears wooden beads in the colors of his clan, so I recognized them immediately.

The two dwarves that entered laughing raucously wore the blue and silver of the Chilox Clan. They looked very much like my father had looked, minus Da's grim expression. Their faces were thin and gaunt, almost elven, and their figures betrayed the same ancestry. Both displayed the same wild look I had seen in my father's eyes, echoing the blaze of the forge.

The older of the two kept a short, well-groomed blond beard, which I had learned was something of a style among lowland dwarves. A mountain dwarf might braid his beard, but he would never trim it. The younger had let his grow wild and had hidden beads and trinkets within its bushy recesses.

The party that strode in with them surprised me more than the appearance of my cousins. They were accompanied by no less than three elves, one male and two female, and as many hoblings, all male as far as I could tell. They sported the long sideburns that were typical of their kind and talked in the high timbered voices that set apart the hoblings.

I was taken aback by my cousins' choice of company. I usually only associated with other dwarves, except when business required, but I was determined to find out what I could about my family.

After buying a bottle of spirits from the barkeep, I made my way up to the group, whose boisterous laughter quieted as I approached.

"Chilox—," I started, unsure of how to explain myself.

"What business do you have with us, brother dwarf?" The smile flashed from the younger man's face as he inquired of me. He was suddenly all business. I noticed the male elf's hand dart to the hilt of his sword as his eyes played uncomfortably over me, no doubt sizing me up, gauging my strengths and weaknesses.

"I am Feldspar Forgehammer of the Clan Forgehammer of Ironfist Forge. My father was Bertram Chilox of your own clan." My words did not have the calming effect that I had hoped. The dwarves' companions still seemed ready for battle.

The older dwarf spoke, "If you wish to regain your clan, it will be difficult, Forgehammer. We only accept those who prove themselves worthy of our line, whether they be born to the clan or no. Our numbers are small after the War of the Bloody Fist, and we won't support anyone who can't pull his own."

"I am an armorsmith by trade," I replied, "and, anyways, I'm not looking for a new family or handouts. I was hoping to hear news of my father and brothers." I placed the bottle of spirits in front of them, but no one relaxed until the older fellow had tried a shot and pronounced it safe to drink.

"I am Hiddukel Chilox," the younger dwarf introduced himself, "and this is Taestiv Chilox. Our companions are Spinner," —he indicated the male elf, who no longer stood guard with his sword, but whose hands glowed with readied magical power— "Puffin and Tephip Lobo," —two of the hoblings tipped their hats—"their cousin Merek," —the other hobling— "and Abbity and Avriel Grandefleur." He finished by pointing at the two females that sat at the table.

"We are House Silversword," he continued, "so named because of our mission: to rid Elysia of Chaos's vile minions, the undead tainters of Tyrra's blood." Tephip produced his sword and laid it on the table. The silver coating on the blade made it shine brightly in the lantern light. Silvering a blade cost a bundle, but I knew it would prove deadly to foes who had risen from the grave with the help of dark necromancy.

"We have heard no news of your family," Taestiv told me. "They left Stonewood some four score summers ago and have not returned since." He exchanged a glance with his brother, and, receiving a nod in return, continued, "We are, however, in need of an armorsmith. Both Hiddukel and I are weaponsmiths, but neither of us can repair or craft armor. Spinner is an excellent salesman. We will provide you with food, shelter, and steel if you outfit our group, and Spinner will sell the excess for the highest price. He'll only take a little bit for his efforts. Won't you, Spinner?"

The elf said nothing, just leaned back and displayed a sly grin that tugged up on one side of his mouth.

So that was how I came to travel with the Silversword, and they taught me how to fight better, and I continued crafting armor for them. Life with the Silversword was immediately different. I was thrust into the role of a warrior, and I began to learn many things about this way of life I had never known. Always in the past, I had allowed others to do the fighting, knowing that their plight was good for my business, but now I was on the front lines, sometimes even asked to battle enemies which I could not harm, just to allow my cousins, and these strange companions of theirs, to escape.

I reluctantly handed over my excess wares to Spinner, but the elf was indeed a fine salesman. He always seemed to know someone who needed what he was selling. He'd trade my armor for potions, those potions for scrolls, scrolls for components used in formal magic, those items for alchemical substances, and then those poisons for gold. Somehow, he always seemed to have a little something left over of each, and far more gold than my armor alone would have fetched.

What else surprised my about the adventuring life was the apparent utilitarian approach to magic. I had always been taught that magic was something to be feared, something that few learned, and those few spent their whole lives learning it. Yet here, it was something that many dabbled in. Both of my cousins could magically close up wounds, as could one of the female elves.

The other elves practiced the magic of the stars. They used it in battle whenever things were not going their way. Nor was this unique to the Silversword. Many such adventuring groups utilized several "battlecasters," many of whom were far more powerful than our own.

I became used to fighting beside the others in House Silversword. Even the hoblings served their purpose. Tephip and Puffin were great at sneaking around behind our enemies and sliding a dagger into their back before the foe knew what was happening. Merek was a battle mage, fighting with a sword and shield, then stepping back to blast the enemy with his sorcery. Together, we hunted down bands of undead creatures and destroyed them and the necromancers who had created them.

I was also spending much of my time at the Stonewood Woodcutters Guild. I was hoping to improve my clan's wealth by apprenticing to this illustrious group. Also, there was a fine dwarf-maiden who I had my eyes on. Her name was Rakella Leafdancer. She was an assistant to Blindor Silverlode, the Guildmistress.

Blindor and the beautiful Rakella had graciously volunteered to teach me how to read and to educate me about the history of Stonewood. Rakella was a few summers older than I. She was slender and athletic. Her hair was a deep earthy brown, and from her chin grew a long braid, reaching down to her waist, where a tiny scarlet ribbon completed it. Her oaken eyes dazzled me, and I must admit I was a poor student because her beauty prevented me from concentrating on her lessons.

I had just arrived one afternoon, carrying the notebook in which I attempted to scrawl the words Rakella taught me, when I was surprised by a commotion within the guildhall. The guildmistress was running around in a huff, and barking orders at the Woodcutters who were there. Rakella looked a mess, her hair disheveled, her eyes red from crying. I ran to her.

"Whatever's the matter?"

"My brother, Rakanel. He's missing." She looked up at me, and the tears threatened to spill once more from their vessels. I felt shameful, but I couldn't prevent myself from noticing the way her chest heaved as she tried to catch her breath between sobs or the way her beautifully full red lips parted just slightly. I looked down at the ground to hide the blood that I felt rushing to my face.

"How can I help, Rakella?" I asked, daring to look back up at those teary eyes.

"Find him, Feldspar. Find him." Looking into those orbs, I felt my heart fill with lead and sink to my feet.

"I will do whatever I can," I responded, "for you." I turned and rushed back to find Hiddukel.

It took no convincing to get my cousins on my side. As soon as they heard that a woodcutter was missing, they rallied together all of the members of the house and readied themselves to join the search.

Rakanel was a Scout for the Woodcutters Guild, so his job was to investigate new areas of the forest to be harvested and to judge the quality of the wood in that region. Scouts would decide whether the trees in an area should be harvested or whether they should be allowed to grow a few more years. Then the Rangers would locate and mark the best trees for harvesting and apply the special chemicals that would soften the wood and allow the Cutters to chop them down.

He had been searching in a new area, one that had been allowed to grow since its previous timbering some fifty years earlier. We gathered up supplies and began the trek out that way, joined by some of the woodcutters.

It wasn't long before Spinner found the dwarf's trail, and we followed it in the fast disappearing light.

In the dark, we began to see strange lights. Little green glows, which came in pairs, stared at us from among the trees. Taestiv drew his sword and made a quick motion with his hand. The others drew their weapons as well, and I my axe, and the hoblings disappeared without a sound.

Hiddukel began pounding on my shield with the flat of his sword, yelling unintelligibly at the darkness. The other dwarves looked at him with concern, and they crept back away from him, so as not to be swept up in his insanity.

"Come and get it!" he yelled. "Come on, buggers!" The lights moved towards us, cautiously at first but speeding up into a full charge. The dwarves moved further away, and began to take defensive stances.

The first creature came into view, and with a yelp it fell to the ground, plowing up the leaves in front of me, a knife protruding from its back. It looked like a wolf, though twice as large as any I had ever seen, and the smell was horrendous. Mucus-filled spit dripped from its gaping maw, and the greenish glow slowly faded from its eyes.

Three others fell before they reached us, the hoblings roguery stopping them mid-charge. Five more broke onto the pathway, snarling with bloodlust. I jumped in front of Hiddukel to shield him from the beasts. Taestiv stepped up beside me, and Hiddukel laid his hands on both of our shoulders, drawing up energy from the earth. His hands began to glow faintly, ready to heal us at a moments notice.

Two of the wolves barreled into our shields, my boots dug into the mud, and the impact almost knocked me over. Their thick hide was difficult to cut through, even with an axe, and it took me several hacks to make the beasts bleed. Meanwhile, they bit and clawed at us. It was all I could do to push them back with the shield.

Taestiv slid his blade under my shield and into the creature that fought us most ferociously. It succumbed to the wounds, and I saw the light fade from its eyes, as it had from the others we killed.

"*I call upon the earth to cure serious wounds,*" Hiddukel chanted, and my own injuries closed up.

Taestiv and I made quick work of the other wolf, and the carnage was over. Our companions had slain all of the creatures.

"Targs," one of the dwarves muttered. "We've seen them lately in the area, though none this close to town. They're wolves, but possessed by some dark power."

"They're like no wolf I've seen," Spinner responded. "Probably what got Leafdancer." He pointed to a tree some fifty yards away. His sharp elven eyes must have spotted something there, but I couldn't see it until I was almost on top of it.

A dwarf lay there, his intestines ripped out and scattered about on the ground around his body. He had been the plaything of these targs. A dwarf indicated that it was indeed the corpse of the man we sought.

"It must have been his final death. May his spirit rest with Tyrra," Taestiv said. "Let's get back, there's nothing more we can do for him." He turned to leave.

"No," the word came unbidden to my lips. "No, I won't leave him here. Take my axe. I'll carry him back to Stonewood."

Taestiv started to protest, but his brother silenced him by taking the axe from my outstretched hand. Spinner helped me lay the body on my shield, and I attached a length of rope to it, a makeshift sledge that I could drag through the forest.

We were attacked again on the return trip, but my mind was elsewhere, so it was fortunate that my strength was not needed for the battle. I thought about Rakella's tears. I thought about the man I dragged behind me. What kind of man was he? Rakella never told me stories about her family, though it was clear from her grieving that she and her brother were close.

It took us twice as long to get back to the Woodcutters Guildhall, but I trudged on, the heavy sledge bouncing on the rocks behind. Rakella met us at the door, and her face instantly fell. She turned back and ran into the hall.

Woodcutters surrounded us, and a few helped me carry Rakanel's body inside. We laid him down on a table inside, and the room was silent. There was no bragging about how many targs we had killed. There was no chuckle of relief at making it safely back. We all stood solemnly around the fallen, knowing that he had been lost forever.

Rakella came to us the next day, her eyes red and dry from crying. She asked me to be the executor of his estate because I had carried his body back. Having agreed, I retrieved Rakanel's death bequest stash using the directions he had left in his sister's care. We arranged to hold his death bequest auction.

Every Stonewood dwarf keeps a stash of unique items or heirlooms in a place only he knows. He writes up a set of directions, using his family's tree as a reference point. A family tree being a stonewood tree marked with the colors of that clan.

In this stash, he'll put anything he finds particularly interesting, such as locks of a relative's beard, beard-growth stones, particularly tasty family recipes, or items which had been passed down to him. Most of these items have fantastic stories attached to them, and the items in Rakanel's death bequest were no different.

Palgor

If the Leafdancer Clan has one weakness, it is a love of gambling and betting. A Leafdancer, some in Stonewood say, would bet you that the sun wouldn't rise tomorrow, if you gave him good enough odds.

Palgor Leafdancer was one of the wealthiest and luckiest dwarves in the town of Stonewood. He was known for holding large shares in the Stonewood Woodcutters Guild, many of which he had won through gambling.

His favorite game was a game of dice, and Palgor loved to drink and dance almost as much as he loved to play dice. While this combination would prove the downfall of many, luck was always on Palgor's side. He won so many wagers that no sober dwarf would play the game against him, unless the bet consisted only of worthless trinkets or clay chips.

Fortunately, Palgor knew he was lucky to have gained so much wealth from a simple game, so he was generous with his fortune and shared it freely. His parties were infamous, and people would talk about them for months afterwards. It was during one of these parties that Palgor's luck turned against him.

Palgor danced and drank. He took no notice of the gypsy who entered and took a seat away from the other guests. Palgor welcomed all visitors at his celebrations, so the man in the black cloak did not immediately draw attention.

The gypsy drew a set of dice out of a pouch and began to fiddle with them, passing them from hand to hand, making them walk across the backs of his fingers.

It wasn't long before a crowd of the fun-loving Leafdancers had gathered around him, throwing gold down onto the table. Every time a dwarf rolled the dice, the man was able to guess the total, or whether the roll would contain two or three of a kind.

"Palgor," called Fingold, Palgor's brother, "you need to check this guy out. He's got better luck than you!"

Palgor waded through the crowd to get a better look at the man who won bet after bet. He watched for a time, trying to figure out the gypsy's secret. Certain there was a trick, but unsure of the method and spurred on by his guests, who were sure Palgor's luck was greater that this man's, Palgor placed a few gold on the table.

The gypsy looked up at the dwarf and drew back his hood. Out of the left side of his face grew nine black gems, glistening in the lantern light.

"I'll not take your gold, brother dvarf." The crowd gasped in surprise at the gypsy's words and looked at Palgor to see his reaction. Most of them expected the dwarf to wind up and slug the man in the nose.

Instead, he simply sat down at the table, stared the gypsy straight in the eye, and added another gold coin to the stack in front of him. The gypsy did not back down. He stared right back into Palgor's stony face.

This exchange continued for two days and two nights, neither man budging, save to answer the call of nature. The stack of gold grew to include all of Palgor's fine jewelry. Soon, Palgor added scraps of paper representing his shares in the Woodcutters Guild and portions of his fortune that he kept in dwarven banks. Still, the gypsy refused to bet with him.

Finally, Palgor secretively scribbled a note on a paper and slid it across the table. The man scanned it, nodded, and produced the dice.

"You vill roll tventy-six," the gypsy predicted. Palgor investigated the dice but could find nothing wrong with their markings or weight. The crowd watched him raise the dice high in the air, give them a thorough shake, and toss them onto the table, one by one, revealing the same total predicted by the mysterious stranger.

Palgor stood slowly, the crowd completely silent. He announced to them that he had lost his entire fortune in the wager. He retired to another room with his now wealthy competitor.

He returned after an hour's discussion, holding only the dice that had cost him his fortune. He did not remain poor very long, however. In truth, the deal he secretly made was to trade his fortune for the gypsy's method of reading the dice. He quickly won back what he had lost by gambling with unsuspecting travelers.

Rakanel Leafdancer bought his uncle's dice at Palgor's death bequest auction, then left them for his own death bequest. In that auction, these "Dice that Paupered Palgor" netted more than thirty gold from a gypsy by the name of Papa Lanesh Kaner. Perhaps he, too, has learned their secret.

Morumbra

I didn't see much of Rakella after her brother's final death. We donated a portion of the proceeds from Rakanel's death bequest auction to the Stonewood Woodcutters Guild. Another portion went to the Leafdancer family, as did those parts of Rakanel's estate not included in the death bequest. I personally withheld Fingold's Twin Stones of Beard Growth from the auction. I use them every day, ribbing them against either side of my face and remembering Rakanel Leafdancer and his father Fingold.

What remained from the money gained at the auction we used, with Rakella's permission, to equip ourselves. Some strange events had occurred in Vindale, the capitol city of the Barony of Woodhaven, the same barony that included the entirety of the Stonewood Forest. We thought there might be some connection between the targs that had killed Rakanel and the shadowy creatures seen around Vindale.

It was only a few hours travel to the city, and the road was straight and well protected by Elysian soldiers. Even so, we traveled with our weapons at the ready, for the stories told by adventurers passing through the city frightened us.

They told us that people's own shadows were attacking them. Creatures came out of any patch of darkness and began clawing at hapless individuals. This, however, was not even the strangest tale. One adventurer told us about an entire building which had appeared out of thin air.

A short jaunt through the woods brought us to the mystical structure. It was a large building made of stone and wood. The door stood open, but the glow just inside the entrance told us a circle of power protected it.

We crouched in the brush, silently planning our course of action. Then we saw it, a wispy figure floating just above the ground, shimmering in the daylight. Could this be one of the shadows that had plagued the city? We continued to hide and watch.

Out of the building, following behind the partially invisible creature, came two that we knew: Lanesh Kaner, the gypsy who had bought Palgor's dice, and Lady Willissa Entemoor, a friend of the Stonewood Woodcutters Guild. I stared into their eyes from my hiding spot, looking for any sign of magical charm or enslavement. They sure acted as if the creature was a friend, though its appearance frightened us, especially given the tales we had heard in town.

Spinner Grandefleur, the elven mage, made a sign to Hiddukel, then moved silently to a new position some distance away from us and back down the main path to town. He started whistling a tune to himself. Whistling! I couldn't believe me ears; surely the creature would hear this. I watched in incredulity as the elf bustled his way up the trail, taking no care to conceal his return.

"Papa Lanesh!" he hailed the gypsy loudly. "My Lady," he added in a quieter, more formal tone, bowing slightly. "I had heard that a building had appeared out of thin air, but I believed it to be rumor. I had no idea that you were behind this trick."

"Vat? Oh! Zis ist no trickink," Lanesh replied in thick gypsy accent. I expected the creature to attack Spinner any moment, but now I understood his plan. The elven race held an innate resistance to being magically charmed and forced to befriend such a creature, and if the shimmering being attacked him with force, it would break any such spell that affected the other two. As the elf approached the group, the conversation continued, no longer so loud that we could hear.

After a few minutes of discussion, Spinner beckoned to us. Hiddukel led the way, standing and striding towards the others. I followed quickly, not wanting any harm to befall my cousin.

"Lanesh tells me this creature is a 'Time Flyer' and a 'Hoylean,' a being that exists in all time, yet no time," Spinner explained to Hiddukel. "It is the antithesis of the 'Morumbrians,' the shadow creatures that have been attacking the town. This building is the Hoylean Library, a collection of documents from the past which the Hoyleans have brought to us in order to fight the Morumbrians."

The starry creature floated towards the building and in through the circle, ignoring the circle of power's presence, which ordinarily stopped entry by even the most powerful of beings. The gypsy followed behind it. He motioned us in, and I felt a tingle of magic as I stepped through the bounds of the circle. Lanesh was obviously "invested" in the circle, which meant that we needed his permission to enter or leave the circle. When he asked us to leave our weapons inside the protective formal magic, I looked apprehensively to my cousin, who simply nodded to indicate that I should follow the gypsy's instructions. I placed my axe in the pile of weapons and followed Lanesh's gesture into the library.

Rows and rows of books sat on shelves around the common room. Several tomes lay upon the table, open for reading. The language on the spines was unfamiliar to me. The strange thing, however, was the lack of dust. Lanesh told us the library was ancient, but the room and all of its contents seemed to have been created just the day before.

In the opposite corner from the entrance, a second circle of power glowed faintly. It was unlike any circle I had seen before. Two concentric circles had been built into the floor, their metallic bands twinkling with stored magical power. In the band created between the circles, several arcane sigils had been placed into the floor. A musical organ stood in the center, bands of energy flowing along its keys and up its small pipes.

I approached the organ and discovered that I could enter the circle despite my lack of investiture. Looking back at the group, I noticed that they were all deep in conversation. I cracked my knuckles and turned to the keys. Prior to this, I had never had much musical experience, but I had watched closely as the Ironfist Forge bards had played the massive stalagmite organs. This keyboard was similar, though smaller and lacking the foot pedals which the dwarves used to produce the deepest bass notes. I reached out to touch a key, but a pale slender hand gripped my wrist.

"Know you what you do, brother?" the voice of Lady Willissa chided me. She used the term that we dwarves used to refer to members of our own race, having earned such a right by the work she had done for the Stonewood Woodcutters Guild. "This instrument is not like other instruments. Allow me to show you." She played a simple melody, and I felt power surge through me as the sigils around the circle began to glow brightly. The light expanded to envelope both of us. Then, in a flash, we were gone.

I looked around to notice that I was in a different, smaller chamber, presumably elsewhere in the library. Rubbing my eyes, I was sure that what I saw was the truth.

"But... how?"

"The organ is harmonically attuned to each of these rooms through an ancient magic, a practice lost to us now. The Hoyleans used it to travel, not just to other places, but to other times."

I looked around in wonder. The room in which we now stood was some kind of musical library. Its walls were lined with instruments of all shapes and sizes. I picked a lute and admired its craftsmanship.

"All of these are Hoylean instruments?" I asked.

"Yes, the Hoyleans taught us how to get to this chamber first. It also contained some musical scores that allowed us to travel to different parts of the library."

Putting down the lute, I asked, "Can you teach me?"

Willissa smiled. "Do you have any musical experience?"

"Some," I lied.

"Then you may become my pupil."

Surprisingly, despite my lack of musical training, I picked up the basics very quickly. I spent most of my time in the Hoylean Library, practicing various travel tunes and studying translations of some of the Hoylean writings. Occasionally, my companions returned to fill me in on details of their battles against the shadows and targs, but, with my cousin's blessing, I rarely left the library to fight alongside them.

Lady Willissa taught me several tunes for which I did not know the purpose, but which I devoured eagerly. It was after I had learned one of these to her satisfaction that she introduced me to the Star Chamber.

She played a tune that I had heard others play, but never experienced for myself. The circle whisked us away to a room I had never seen. It looked unlike any other room in the library. The walls curved around us, and I could not tell where the ceiling began and the walls ended or where the walls began and the floor ended. The room appeared to be built out of the blackest marble, but floating in the marble were millions of tiny points of light.

"This is the Star Chamber," the elf explained. "It is, in truth, the body of a Hoylean who has transcended our plane of existence. Each of these points of light represents a different time and place in our history. We can use them to travel to those moments."

I looked around at the countless stars that surrounded me. "How do you know which light takes you to which moment?"

She smiled and moved my hands to the organ keys. "Play your newest tune for me, the Ballad of Ringold and Nephtali."

I obeyed, starting into the long tune. My fingers growing more comfortable with the music as I continued to play. The runes around me began to glow, but their light never grew so bright that they eclipsed the stars surrounding us. Then, as I neared the end of the tune, I noticed a movement. One of the lights began to vibrate with the tune.

"Keep playing," Willissa insisted, and I noticed that I had paused briefly in my recitation of the song. I redoubled my efforts, playing with feverish anticipation. The wiggling light grew brighter and larger, as if it were coming nearer. Its color changed from white to blue to red. As I finished the tune, I expected it to retreat again, but, to my astonishment, it remained large and close and continued to vibrate in harmony with the echoes of the song that now faded from the organ pipes.

"Grab my hand," the good lady instructed, and I did as I was told. She reached out toward the moving star. Her fingers met no resistance as they impossibly took hold of the light. A red glow infused itself down her arm and quickly embraced us both. Then in a flash, we stood upon spring grass and could hear the chirping of birds. The sun was starting to set behind the trees.

"This is the Horningwood Forest, many generations ago," Willissa informed me.

"Horningwood? You mean Stonewood?" I asked.

"It's the Horningwood Forest before it became Stonewood." Then, looking down a path between the trees, she added, "Here they come. Let's hide." We secreted ourselves in some brush nearby as a troupe of armored dwarves approached. They entered the clearing and stopped for some rest.

"Shall we camp here for the night, Sire?" asked a man who wore a captain's insignia. He must have been the second in command.

"Nay, Argen, we move out after a brief rest. I plan to make it back to Lodestone Mountain tonight."

"Very well, My Liege."

I whispered to Lady Willissa, "Is that–Is that Ringold?" The tremor in my voice betrayed my trepidation and anxiety. The elf simply nodded and continued to watch. The dwarves clustered in the center of the clearing and began to eat some of their rations.

After a quarter hour of rest, the dwarves prepared their packs again. They were getting ready to leave! This wasn't how it was supposed to happen! Ringold had to go for a stroll and meet Nephtali! I urgently whispered my fears to the elf beside me.

"Shhh! We musn't be seen. We musn't interfere with the past!" came her scolding reply.

Fed up, I burst from my hiding spot and walked as quickly and purposefully as I could toward the dwarves who were now ready to set out. Confusion turned to anger and worry as they saw my beaded face bearing down on them.

"Wait!" I called, "you can't go! You need to stay here." I found myself surrounded by the soldiers in the blink of an eye, no less than a dozen drawn blades pushing into my skin through my cloak.

"Who are ye?" "How dare ye?" "Go no further!" The angered men shouted queries and orders at me in a jumble of chaos. Several hands began to glow as sorcerers drew energy from the earth and stars. One magicker and a beefy warrior leapt in front of the king to protect him.

Raising my hands to display their emptiness, I swallowed hard. What trouble had I caused now? Surely Willissa's entreaties had been wise, but my headstrong attitude had brought action before careful consideration once more. Two soldiers pushed the elf forward into my view.

"This pointy-ear was with him, Sire, no others," the captain informed his lord. Willissa looked distraught and disappointed. I bowed my head to hide my guilty eyes from her stricken gaze.

"How come ye to steal upon us without notice?" Ringold addressed me directly, stepping out from behind his living shield. He was a majestic dwarf, standing taller than any of his men, his beard a fine golden mane that he had braided and wrapped three times around his waist. Bejeweled gold rings held the braid in place, matching the jewelry that adorned his fingers and ears. His hair was the same maple color as his beard and he wore it in a long braid down his back. His face revealed strength of resolve but also a kindness that contradicted the battle-scars on his bare right forearm. His left arm was covered in chain and plate. A sword clanked at his hip as he walked forward, the sapphire in its hilt dazzlingly beautiful.

"I—We were here, Sire." My tongue swelled inside my parched mouth, unwilling to pollute the king's ears with its scratchy timbre.

"An ambush, then? Not very successful." The lord chuckled at his joke, and the men relaxed their death glare, though the blades still pushed in on me.

"No, Sire," I pressed on. "We are friends. I—I am a Stonewood dwarf like yourself."

"Stonewood?" All the dwarves gave me a quizzical look. "What is this 'Stonewood'?"

"Horningwood, I mean, Horningwood, Sire."

"A spy, then. A poor, idiot spy who failed to learn even the name of the kingdom he was to infiltrate, and one who went charging in to the arms of his captors." The men laughed at my misfortune.

"No, Sire," I grasped for something that could convince him I was no spy. "I—I'm a—a Seer," I blurted out, remembering the runestones that some folk swore by. "I divined your passage in the stones, and I wanted to make sure you didn't make a mistake."

Ringold looked thoughtfully at me for a moment, then responded with a barely audible whisper, "What mistake?"

"The mistake of leaving here without meeting your intended love."

"Ha! A man lays in wait with a pointy-eared woman, then comes barging out of a bush to tell me I am to meet my queen!" He and his men laughed raucously at the insinuation. "I suppose this elf-woman is her?" He turned to Willissa, bowing low in mockery, "My Queen, I am enchanted by your beauty!" He brought a hand to his forehead. "I am stricken! Aah!" He pretended to faint into his captain's arms.

"Not her, you fool!" The blades renewed their tension on my skin at the insult. "The one you are to meet later this night!" Willissa's eyes met mine and betrayed the hurt and anger she felt. I was filled with dejection. Could I do nothing right? I saw her hand reach down for her focus, hoping to save us by beating a quick retreat to our own time. Looking down, I started at the sight that met me, a single white lily sprouted from the ground at the elf's feet. Instantly, I knew what to do. I burst into song, my arid voice beginning flat and soft, but finding the right tone quickly and gaining in volume as my courage increased. I sang the song of Ringold and Nephtali.

Lady Willissa added her voice to mine, and she and I both reached for the magic with our minds, the magic of the song. The forest was alive with it, and the energy flowed through us in waves that mimicked the rhythm of the tune. The birds added their chirps and whistles. Leaves rustled in time. Wind blew a droning hum through the branches. The soldiers stood entranced and relaxed their grips. The elf was able to reach into her bag and pull out a small harp for accompaniment.

When the song ended, the forest resonated. The dwarves, however, stood in silent awe. King Ringold regarded me with a new expression. He was the first to break the silence.

"Tie them up," he said in a quiet voice. The men were slow to act, and Willissa and I wondered that the song had been so full of magic and power, yet had apparently not worked to our advantage. Then, I heard the king's second command and understood that it had been effective. "Make camp. We stay here tonight."

I felt rough hands grab me and pull my hands behind my back where cords were wound around my wrists. I watched as the captain approached Willissa, who revealed her grace and strength of will by dropping the harp and allowing the dwarf to bind her hands without protest. A dirty kerchief prevented me from talking or singing. The king himself offered his own spider-silk handkerchief for Lady Willissa's gag. The soldiers escorted us to the center of the clearing and prepared their camp around us. Several dwarves stood sentry far from the site.

Ringold stared at us from a distance, talking to his captain. His furrowed brow showed concern though we could obviously cause him no harm, bound as we were. I wished I could read his thoughts, or at least hear his conversation. The captain turned and came to stand guard over us. The king shook his head and walked down the path into the setting sun.

A hearty greeting awoke me. It was dark, close to midnight judging by the stars. I rubbed my head where it ached from the packed earth on which it lay, taking a moment to realize that my hands were free. I reached up to find that my gag had been removed as well. Sitting up, I looked around at the joyful scene that surrounded me.

The dwarves were sitting around the fire, each with a mug, bottle, or flask in his hand. I could hear their gruff voices raised in song. A celebration. What were they celebrating?

"Har har!" The dwarf who had awakened me offered his wineskin. "You were right, lad. We celebrate our master's lovely bride."

"What? So fast?" I asked, incredulous at the events.

"Well, a good dwarf woos women fast and strong!" the soldier chuckled. "He says you must be quite a Seer, to know that a woman of such beauty awaited him." I looked around, but did not see the king. As if reading my thoughts, the man continued, "He won't even return to camp tonight. She must be gorgeous!"

Looking to my left, I saw Willissa had joined in drinking and conversation with the dwarves. At least they were quick to forgive. I joined the troupe in singing and emptying bottles. The soldiers, who had been partying before we awoke, ended their reverie early, and Willissa and I returned to our own time, not without the elf giving me a scathing directive to never interfere with another part of history.

Though I argued that my indiscretion caused Ringold to stop at that place in the Horningwood Forest and meet Nephtali, Willissa insisted that my meddling could have fouled things up for all of us. She didn't allow me to travel with the others to any other times, so I had to satisfy myself with hearing accounts of all the discoveries they made and the battles they fought. By this time, my study of Harmonic Magic made me useful to the group, even without traveling with them. Every traveler used a "focus" to bring them back to our time, and it was my job to attune each focus through song, as well as to assist new travelers in finding their foci. Merek and Spinner, being magic users and scholars, were eager to learn about the ancient magics and experience time travel.

"There's a fellow from Simoondale, has learned a magic called 'Shadowbane' from the ancients," Merek told Spinner and me, looking up from his work. "Says it's really effective against the Morumbrians. One spell can destroy, or at least banish, even a powerful shadow." Merek shaped a wolf's head out of clay to make his temporary focus. It took some experience in time travel before an adventurer could create a permanent focus by enchanting a more permanent object than a clay shape. Permanent foci were far superior to the temporary clay models, which were crafted in a form discovered in the void that existed between times. If a clay focus broke due to accident or the rigors of battle, it would rip the traveler out of time and return him to the star-chamber from whence he left. A permanent focus also had the advantage of being able to carry multiple adventurers, as Willissa and I had done, for I had no focus of my own, temporary or permanent.

"Too bad 'Shadowbane' doesn't work in our time, then," Spinner reminded us that we had to contend with the Morumbrian shadows in the present as well as the past.

"Well," I said, looking up from the new tune I was studying, "the Hoyleans insist that defeating the Morumbrians in all times is the only way to be rid of them in any time."

Spinner mentioned more good news. "Our ancient Hoylean friends are teaching Papa Lanesh something called 'Entropic Magic.' He says it'll allow people to sprout claws and body weapons by partially devolving into beasts. That'll make our fighting force stronger."

I nodded. It was difficult to fight the shadows in the past, because only certain items, such as foci, traveled with us. No weaponry came along, and, though weapons could often be obtained from the time to which we traveled, the more powerful Morumbrians were unaffected by ordinary blades.

"Several people have been working on unlocking the Hoylean Armory, myself included," I told my friends. "It's said to contain all manner of 'Light' and 'Shadowbane' weapons that can travel. That should allow us non-magickers to be of some service. We just can't get the tune right," I said, shaking my head, remembering frustrating hours spent practicing at that tune and meeting only disappointment when playing it would not take me to the armory.

"You're a 'magicker' at heart, Feldspar," Merek chortled, his slender face shaking with laughter. "You spend hours here, slaving over some new song or bit of history. Remember when you and I discovered the key to translating that note held by one of the Morumbrian spies? By the stars, it was you who first uttered the word 'Morumbra.' Other warriors just want to kill things. You study, study, study, more than most scholars I know." I smiled back at him. Trust a hobling to know just how to cheer a body up.

"What's this?" Spinner pointed at the page he was reading, a translation of some Hoylean records. His brow pressed together in concentration. He passed the parchment across the table so that Merek could look at it.

"The three weapons have proven to be too erratic," the hobling read aloud for my benefit, "probably due to their sentience. Therefore, they have been taken away from the main library site so that they cannot fall into the wrong hands. The spirits within the blades has given them great power, especially when traveling through times, as they gain even greater power when certain alignments of the stars and planets have been noted. If the power could be harnessed, these swords would be more powerful than any ever created. It is unlikely, however, that this will ever be a viable option of enchanting weapons, as the power, left unchained, would drive the wielder of such a weapon to insanity. Perhaps the passage of time will decrease the strength of the blades' inner souls to a point where they could be safely used for long periods of time. Hopefully, this will be the case, as these enchantments may be our only hope in defeating our Auld Enemy." Merek scanned down the page further. "Says here that one of the swords, 'Mora'Dûm,' was hidden in a chamber in the Horningwood Forest. I know I know that name from somewhere."

"The Horningwood Forest was the original name for the Stonewood Forest," I informed him, looking through them both. Mora'Dûm, a blade of great power, power that could be used to defeat our enemy, was hidden somewhere near my hometown. The lines from the text echoed in my mind: "…these enchantments may be our only hope in defeating our Auld Enemy."

"Merek, Spinner," I looked from one to the other, "We need to find that blade." I stood up quickly, ready to take action.

"Not so fast, Fo-ham," Spinner said as he grabbed me by the arm, knowing that the friendly nickname would ease my fired spirit. "You must follow the way of the scholar. Ignore that fighting instinct within you and study. We must find out all we can about that blade, where it's hidden, and what we will face when we get there. That is the scholar's way."

As books and records would not contain my adventuring spirit for long, we started out the next day. I had not gotten much sleep, having stayed awake pouring over translation after translation, hoping to find some other mention of Mora'Dûm and the other "sentient" blades. I felt more anxious than I usually did before setting out, my senses heightened by the excitement of doing something to help in the war against Morumbra and by worry. The warning about the instability and volatility of the weapons weighed heavy on my mind, lightened only slightly by the Hoylean belief that time would weaken their power. The journey to Stonewood from Vindale was not long, both were in the Barony of Woodhaven, but my mind wandered during the trip, casting doubt on the venture one moment, urging me on with hope the next.

What did the text mean by calling the weapons "sentient?" The term implied that the weapons were awake, conscious of their surroundings, yet how could a piece of steel be capable of feeling and perception? Sure, I knew from smithing that the metal spoke to a metalworker in its own way. A skilled smith could look at a bar of steel, heft it in his hand, and know whether it would make a fine quality blade or something of middling quality, suitable for general trade, or even whether the metal should be cast away, good only for an apprentice's practice. However, the metal did not know about its potential, the knowledge was the craftsman's. Even watching the bend of the metal as it heated and the colors that formed in its surface would tell the smith what to do with the piece, but, while older masters would call this sense the "Song of Steel" and say the metal spoke or sang to them, the lore actually came from the worker's instincts, as finely forged as any blade by decades shaping iron. I still could not understand how a sword could gain, or even mimic, true sentience.

When we arrived in Stonewood, Merek guided us deep into the heart of the old forest, where his reading had led him to believe we would find the hidden blade. His studies must have been more thorough than mine, for they led us to a cave hidden by underbrush and tall stonewood trees that had, obvious by their size, never been cut. After some effort in clearing away the brush, we were able to enter the cave. Passageways went in all directions, and we split up momentarily to investigate.

"Hey, look at this," Spinner called from a side tunnel, raising the glowing orb of his light spell so that we could see the chamber upon which he had stumbled. The far side of the room—for it was indeed a room crafted by people's hands—disappeared in darkness. Black marble pillars spanned from the floor to the vaulted ceiling. Approaching the opposite side of the chamber, we came upon a wide stone door, braced with metal.

"This is dwarven craftsmanship," I surmised, noting the runes carved into the door. "These runes, they are old, but definitely Tokai." Brushing away dust with my hands, I read the sigils. "May he who enters here be strong of spirit and pure of heart. He who prizes the power locked within must battle with the earth itself. He who succeeds shall be the heir to the power of Mora'Dûm." I told no one about the special significance that I saw in the lily that was carved into the gateway beside the runes.

Silence surrounded me. No one dared breathe. I reached forward to the handle of the door, knowing that my destiny awaited me inside.

A hand stopped mine. A thin elven hand... Spinner.

"Feldspar," he smiled gently, "I know you feel it is your duty to face this first, but there are those here who are stronger and more experienced than you, and those knowledgeable in the magical arts. Please, allow someone else to step up to this challenge."

I nodded slowly and followed Spinner's gesture to a place beside the great door, standing ready to defend my compatriots should some menace vault itself from behind the portal. Merek stepped forward first, slowly approaching the entrance to the second chamber. Taking hold of the great handle, he pulled the door open. It opened into a smaller room, with nothing inside save a table. Upon the table sat a single sword.

"Mora'Dûm," I gasped, and I heard others uttering the same behind me. Merek approached the sword. As he entered the room, orbs above him began to glow with magical power. He looked back at us warily, but nothing more happened to startle us. He sheathed his own sword and readied his shield.

When he reached down to pick up Mora'Dûm, a red spark enveloped his hand. The doors slammed shut, separating us from aiding him. I ran forward, pulling at the handles, pounding on the stone, but I could not open the gateway, nor could my shouting be heard over the rumble that emanated from the second chamber. The rumbling finally stopped and we could hear a faint echo of battle sounds and Merek's voice casting magic. Then, silence. The doors slowly swung open and there lay our hobling friend, battered and wounded. Upon the table, the sword glistened with blood red light.

After healing Merek, another adventurer stepped up to battle the Earth Elemental that the hobling told us lay in wait. One by one, adventurers stepped up, fought, and fell. Soon, all of the others had attempted, and eyes turned to me.

I walked forward with steadfast resolve. I would not allow the creature to best me. Mora'Dûm must be torn from its clutches so that we could use it against the Morumbrians. I entered the smaller room and reached for the sword. A spark and the doors were shut. The floor beneath me growled thunderously. The quake knocked me off my feet as the marble buckled and bent. A pillar of stone shot out from the ground and began to take the shape of a man. I pulled myself up, using the table for support. Before me stood a marble warrior, seven feet tall, broad in shoulder, a perfect specimen of masculinity. His hands were as big as my head, and sharp, jeweled claws sprouted from each digit.

Its eyelids, which had been closed up to this point, suddenly sprang open to glare at me with glittering emeralds that burned with inner light. The stone man extended his claws toward me, a sound escaping his throat like the roar of an avalanche.

The creature and I circled around each other looking for gaps in each other's defenses. I began to wonder how it was possible to harm a boulder. A thought floated to the top of my mind, but was displaced as I rolled to avoid the creature's swipe.

Something I had seen in Ironfist Forge rankled on my brain, but I had never seen anyone battle an elemental. I shook my head as I parried a set of blows aimed at my chest. Then the vision came clearly to me. Miners. I had watched the miners dangling from the cliff-face working together to pull huge hunks of rock and ore from the seam.

"They look for imperfections in the rock," I heard the foreman's voice in my head. "Even if a stone is harder than steel, a miner can tell where to aim his pick, where the weak points are, and if it'll tend to crack this way or that."

As the warrior approached me again, I looked for any weakness, any sign of imperfection. I had to leap out of the way as the flurry of blows renewed. Looking down at my shield, I wondered how long it would stand up to this battering. I backed across the room, trying to put some distance between me and my attacker.

I realized my mistake as his hand began to glow. A green gem appeared in his palm, and I tried to avoid it as it rocketed towards me, knowing that it was a Stone Bolt spell. It caught the trailing edge of my shield and enveloped me with emerald light, crushing my insides. My armor cracked under the strain. I gasped for breath, but the pain was gone in a flash.

I closed the gap to my foe. He would defeat me easily if I allowed him to stand back and pummel me with magic. I had no way of harming him from that distance. Only by the sword could I hope to beat him. I feinted and struck, driving him back with powerful, deliberate slashes. He clawed at me, and I parried. Blocking his second strike on my shield, I noticed something to give me hope. A vein of weaker quarts extended across his torso.

I blocked a strike and rolled to avoid another and bring me in line with his weak point. As I cut across, Mora'Dûm's blade sparked fiercely. The creature moved down and back to avoid the sword, and I thought I would miss my target. There was a flash of light and Mora'Dûm struck, biting into the seam.

Astonished that I'd hit where I intended despite the elemental's dodge, I didn't move out of the way in time. Pain and blood exploded from my shoulder where his claws tore through my armor. The warrior's spiteful roar rattled my head. He struck back fiercely, and I struggled to parry the blows. For a moment, I thought he had knocked the sword out of my hand, but with a flash Mora'Dûm was back in my grip.

I pushed toward my foe, moving on the offensive, quickly striking out at my target. Again and again Mora'Dûm struck true, exactly where I intended. I knew I was fighting better than I ever had, the blade's magic pumping through me. With a final deafening roar and a brilliant green flash, the beast crumbled to dust and the gateway reopened.

I was only vaguely aware of Spinner's ministrations as he bandaged my wounds. My attention focused on the sword as I examined it for the first time. Mora'Dûm was a longsword of average length. Its hilt was plain with an unadorned steel pommel and red leather stretched across the handle. A short, simple crossguard separated the handle from the blade. Tendrils of blood red copper flame licked up from the base of Mora'Dûm's blade, the rest of which was forged of blackened steel. It was from this fiery ornamentation that the bursts of magical power emanated. I felt the sword's energy pulse in my hand, and, inexplicably, I felt a thirst, a longing, to taste again the power I had felt while fighting the elemental. I also felt a strange desire to keep the weapon for myself, though I knew it would serve our cause much better in the hands of a more skilled warrior.

Our return to Vindale was uneventful. Bolstered by a sense of heroism, I strode to my cousins' Vindale residence with my head high. Hiddukel and Taestiv grinned broadly as they answered our call. I thought perhaps news of our adventure had preceded us. I couldn't help feeling a little disappointed that I would not be the one to share the good tidings. I also could not help but feel a little resentment that one of them would get the sword. I had won Mora'Dûm. It should be mine.

"Brother Fo'ham!" Taestive greeted me as he clasped my forearm, his smile so wide it split his face in two. "Hiddukel has been invited to join the peerage of Elysia. He will be named Baron of Woodhaven!"

I gasped at the unexpected announcement. The peerage were the commoners who were granted lands and titles that put them on the same level as nobility.

Hiddukel addressed the entire group. "Henceforth, I will no longer be leading House Silversword. Those who wish to follow me can do so under a new banner, that of House Woodhaven."

"Then, my liege," I raised me voice so all could hear, "allow me to present to you a tithe." I knelt and held out Mora'Dûm's hilt before me, though it pained me to offer up the fine blade.

"No, Feldspar," Hiddukel said as he laid his hand on my shoulder, "I have heard of your quest to find the sentient weapon. Your new sword will serve me better in your hands, with you as my Lord Seneschal. Besides, I suspect a weapon of that power, especially one rumored to have a mind of its own, would have bound itself to the warrior who freed it from its confinement." My thoughts flicked back to the battle with the elemental, when the sword had flashed back to my grip after being disarmed. What Hiddukel said was true. I felt momentarily ashamed that I had almost inadvertently humiliated him. If he had tried to take the sword, but it jumped back into my hands… But then the meaning of his other statement struck me. He was going to make me Seneschal. That meant that I would not only record important events and meetings for him, but I would also fill in for him at those events that he could not attend. I had not known that my cousin trusted me so much. I would have to make sure that trust was not misplaced.

Trust in me seemed to return in all respects after I made my triumphant appearance with Mora'Dûm. Lady Willissa allowed me to accompany the others on raids against the Morumbrians back in time. I received my own focus, and Mora'Dûm came with me whenever I went, his magic directing my strikes to my foes' most critical spots. I grew to love the feeling of power that the sword brought me. Not only was it extremely light and easy to swing, it also imparted some of its magic directly to me so that I had my first taste of casting spells. The spell in Mora'Dûm's heart was called Amalzix's Mystic Bombardment. It allowed me to shoot small magic bolts from my hands indefinitely as long as I concentrated on holding the spell and did not try to walk. I used the spell whenever I had a chance. It made me feel a strength that owed nothing to my muscles. The power coursed through me like lightning, and I felt my breath come quicker and my heart pound faster. I only wished for more.

Thus, it was in my one-hundred twentieth year that I asked a talented magician to perform the strong magics that would transform me, allowing me to forget the skills I knew and open up a path in which I could learn to be a spellcaster in my own right. The power I felt while using Mora'Dûm was now mine to own. Still it came as quite a shock when my precious blade failed me in battle, and I was struck unconscious.

Mora'Dûm

I only saw Mora'Dûm's blade cleaved in half by the orc that stood before me, then blackness. I spiraled down into the blackness, the shattered weapon falling before me. The wind was knocked out of me as I struck a hard surface. Mora'Dûm clattered to the floor, a mess of lifeless, broken steel, its glow now gone. I wanted to rest. My muscles ached from battle. My head ached from concentrating on difficult spells.

"I am sorry to have failed you," a voice said in the darkness. It was an unfamiliar voice, elven by the accent, perhaps a dark elf. "My master never intended the enchantment to last as long as it did, but those Hoyleans kept it alive with one of their 'Stasis bubbles.' I have enjoyed being out in the world once more, able to battle."

I looked around, but could not see my own hands, let alone the speaker. "Who are you?"

"Oh, I'm sorry, do you need light?" the voice taunted me. "*I grant you the power of a Light.*" Upon the casting of the spell, a miniature moon appeared in the dark elf's hand. Yes, it was indeed a dark elf. He wore only black. The only thing about his that was not that color was his silver hair, which peaked out from under a head scarf, and his scarlet belt. He walked a circle around me. "I am surprised that a weak dwarven mind like yours has been able to learn so much magic of the Celestial School. It is rare, you know. Of course you know," he chuckled, "it is your own feebleminded people of which I speak."

I felt anger well up within me, but my body was so sore I could do naught about it.

"Ah, yes, your temper, something your race is famous for," he continued. "I can see you are angry with me. You believe I, Mora'Dûm, have failed you, that I have brought you here to taunt you. Truthfully, I have brought you here to tell you my story. This is my final death, but you will live on, so I want you to be able to spread this tale. Sit still, Feldspar. It is your time to listen.

"My master was a great experimenter of magic. He was also a great teacher. He rarely took apprentices, so when my father heard that he was going to take on four young students, I was rushed to the line of youth that gathered for his consideration. He only asked each hopeful for a name, and hushed anyone who volunteered more. When he heard my name, he pulled me aside, and soon I stood with three others of his choosing. We traveled to his laboratory. There, he began to teach us about magic.

"The master also told us about his own apprenticeship, how he had been the student of a very great teacher named Sunlev'gantano. I was puzzled at first, for this was how we knew our own master. He explained that Sunlev'gantano was a ceremonial name, given to the one who was most likely to bring about the new order. I was frightened, did he mean an overthrow of civilization? No, my brother dwarf, he meant the height of civilization: the Order of the Sun, a group that crossed all times and all cultures, a society led by the wisest philosophers, a world of plenty and peace.

"I wanted so much to belong to this order and become, as my master had become, the Sunbringer, Sunlev'gantano. Can you imagine, a society where the most intelligent rule? Where magicians finally get the respect they deserve?"

I felt the time was right to speak. "Sorcerers do get respect, dark elf. I have had naught but good treatment since I learned magic."

"Ah, but it is still strength of arm that matters. It is time for magicians to break free, to form their own perfect society."

"How? By subjugating the innocent?" I could not control the disgust in my voice.

"If need be!" His fierce tone took me aback. "Why shouldn't the smartest rule? I suppose you have some ignorant notion that the weak should be protected. You're as silly as that simpleton that our master decided to pass the title to.

"I had to kill him, you understand. I had to gain my master's favor, and Takei was too loved." I heard the pain in the dark elf's voice. Was he about to cry? "My master loved Takei. He was, like you, an idealist. He believed that people should live in harmony, not one over the other, and for that, Master loved him more. I had to kill him. I could not think of any other way. I pushed him off a cliff while we were out gathering magical components.

"My master found out that I did it, and he sentenced me to a life of misery. I did not know it at the time. I thought only that he wanted to try some new spell on me. But he killed me, killed me and trapped my spirit in that sword." He pointed at the remains of Mora'Dûm that littered the floor and shuddered before taking a deep breath to regain his composure. "Well, that is past, and now I am vindicated. My master told me that my imprisonment in the weapon would bring the sun and destroy the shadow. I thought that meant I would be named Sunlev'gantano."

"But you see," I countered, "your imprisonment did destroy the shadow. I helped defeat the Morumbrians with Mora'Dûm—with you."

He grinned slightly on the side of his thin lips. "I guess, then, that I am the Sunbringer after all. Anyway, I was also told to hold on to one secret until my final death. Now I share that secret with you."

I put aside any thought of disgust to hear the man's final words. "Share it, and I will keep it."

"No, it's not to be kept. It's to be spread. You must spread the secret."

I nodded.

"There," he began, pausing for several breaths, "is no Order of the Sun. There is no order and no perfect society, nor will there ever be." A tear crept down the side of his face.

"There will be," I replied. "There will be, and I will bring it, but the premise is flawed. A perfect society requires learning from each other and being considerate of one another's ideals, not a tyranny of the learned elite."

"There is one last thing," he said, ignoring my statement. He reached into the front of his smock and withdrew a small white lily.

I heard his goodbye as the darkness brightened and I regained consciousness, "Farewell. Sunlev'gantano."

Epilogue

Some time after that, my cousin was deposed as Baron of Woodhaven. He was loved by commoners, and I have yet to fully understand his wrongdoing. He was only recently cleared as an outlaw and permitted to return to Elysia. I also have left, traveling and studying magic. The power drives me. In addition, the desire to learn as much as I can about different societies drives me, in the hope that one day I can help bring about the creation of the perfect society envisioned by Sunlev'gantano. I gather stories from each culture, and finally I understand that a perfect society cannot limit itself to one race or one class of people. A perfect society requires learning from each other and being considerate of one another's ideals.

Having freed myself of the racism and hatred that plagued me in my younger years, I was freed also of the name Crimson. I've taken the name Feldspar, the name of that dwarf who saw potential within me. Yet, I am still the crimson dwarf. My hands are bloody, if only in defending those I love. For that reason, I hold onto the name as a reminder that one must accept others on the basis of their abilities, not their external features. I am reminded of the Crimson Clan, which hated outsiders so much that they, themselves, became outsiders. Let us not be like them. Let us follow the sun to enlightenment.

Made in the USA
Charleston, SC
27 June 2012